Also by Lydia Davis

STORIES

Varieties of Disturbance
Samuel Johnson Is Indignant
Almost No Memory
Story and Other Stories
Sketches for a Life of Wassilly
The Thirteenth Woman and Other Stories

NOVEL

The End of the Story

SELECTED TRANSLATIONS

Swann's Way by Marcel Proust
Hélène by Pierre Jean Jouve
Rules of the Game, I: Scratches by Michel Leiris
The Spirit of Mediterranean Places by Michel Butor
The Madness of the Day by Maurice Blanchot
Death Sentence by Maurice Blanchot

Break It Down

BREAK IT DOWN

Stories by

LYDIA DAVIS

Farrar · Straus · Giroux

New York

FARRAR, STRAUS AND GIROUX
18 West 18th Street, New York 10011

Many of the stories in this book were previously published in the
following collections by Lydia Davis: The Thirteenth Woman
(Living Hand, 1976); Story and Other Stories (The Figures,
1983). "Sketches for a Life of Wassilly" was first published by
Station Hill Press in 1981. Grateful acknowledgment is also made
to Fiction International, Luna Tack, Oink!, and The Paris
Review, where some of these stories first appeared. "The Sock"
originally ran in several newspapers, in slightly different form,
under the sponsorship of the PEN Syndicated Fiction Project.
"Extracts from a Life" is adapted from Nurtured by Love by
Shinichi Suzuki, and is used by permission of Exposition Press.
The tale in "Once a Very Stupid Man" is adapted from the
traditional Hasidic story recounted in Martin Buber's The Way of
Man, and is used by permission of Citadel Press.

The Library of Congress has cataloged the hardcover edition as follows:
Davis, Lydia, 1947–
    Break it down : stories / by Lydia Davis
    p. cm.
    ISBN-10: 0-374-11653-9
    I. Title.

    PS3554.A9356 B74 1986
    813'.54—dc19

                86007687

Paperback ISBN-13: 978-0-374-53144-7
Paperback ISBN-10: 0-374-53144-7

www.fsgbooks.com

3   5   7   9   10   8   6   4

Contents

——

Break It Down

Story

I get home from work and there is a message from him: that he is not coming, that he is busy. He will call again. I wait to hear from him, then at nine o'clock I go to where he lives, find his car, but he's not home. I knock at his apartment door and then at all the garage doors, not knowing which garage door is his—no answer. I write a note, read it over, write a new note, and stick it in his door. At home I am restless, and all I can do, though I have a lot to do, since I'm going on a trip in the morning, is play the piano. I call again at ten-forty-five and he's home, he has been to the movies with his old girlfriend, and she's still there. He says he'll call back. I wait. Finally I sit down and write in my notebook that when he calls me either he will then come to me, or he will not and I will be angry, and so I will have either him or my own anger, and this might be all right, since anger is always a great comfort, as I found with my husband. And then I go on to write, in the third person and the past tense, that clearly she always needed to have a love even if it was a complicated love. He calls back before I have time to finish writing all this down. When he calls, it is a little after eleven-thirty. We argue until nearly twelve. Everything he says is a contradiction: for example, he says he did not want to see me because he wanted to work and even more because he wanted to be alone, but he has not worked and he has not been alone. There is no way I can get him to reconcile any of his contradictions, and when this conversation begins to sound too much like many I had with my husband I say goodbye and hang up. I finish writing down what I started to write down even though by now it no longer seems true that anger is any great comfort.

I call him back five minutes later to tell him that I am sorry about all this arguing, and that I love him, but there is no answer. I call again five minutes later, thinking he might have walked out to his garage and walked back, but again there is no answer. I think of driving to where he lives again and looking for his garage to see if he is in there working, because he keeps his desk there and his books and that is where he goes to read and write. I am in my nightgown, it is after twelve and I have to leave the next morning at five. Even so, I get dressed and drive the mile or so to his place. I am afraid that when I get there I will see other cars by his house

that I did not see earlier and that one of them will belong
to his old girlfriend. When I drive down the driveway
I see two cars that weren't there before, and one of them
is parked as close as possible to his door, and I think
that she is there. I walk around the small building to
the back where his apartment is, and look in the window: the light is on, but I can't see anything clearly
because of the half-closed venetian blinds and the steam
on the glass. But things inside the room are not the same
as they were earlier in the evening, and before there was
no steam. I open the outer screen door and knock. I
wait. No answer. I let the screen door fall shut and I
walk away to check the row of garages. Now the door
opens behind me as I am walking away and he comes
out. I can't see him very well because it is dark in the
narrow lane beside his door and he is wearing dark
clothes and whatever light there is is behind him. He
comes up to me and puts his arms around me without
speaking, and I think he is not speaking not because he
is feeling so much but because he is preparing what he
will say. He lets go of me and walks around me and
ahead of me out to where the cars are parked by the
garage doors.

As we walk out there he says "Look," and my name,
and I am waiting for him to say that she is here and also
that it's all over between us. But he doesn't, and I have
the feeling he did intend to say something like that, at
least say that she was here, and that he then thought

better of it for some reason. Instead, he says that everything that went wrong tonight was his fault and he's
sorry. He stands with his back against a garage door
and his face in the light and I stand in front of him with
my back to the light. At one point he hugs me so suddenly that the fire of my cigarette crumbles against the
garage door behind him. I know why we're out here
and not in his room, but I don't ask him until everything
is all right between us. Then he says, "She wasn't here
when I called you. She came back later." He says the
only reason she is there is that something is troubling
her and he is the only one she can talk to about it. Then
he says, "You don't understand, do you?"

I try to figure it out.
So they went to the movies and then came back to
his place and then I called and then she left and he called
back and we argued and then I called back twice but he
had gone out to get a beer (he says) and then I drove
over and in the meantime he had returned from buying
beer and she had also come back and she was in his room
so we talked by the garage doors. But what is the truth?
Could he and she both really have come back in that
short interval between my last phone call and my arrival
at his place? Or is the truth really that during his call to
me she waited outside or in his garage or in her car and
that he then brought her in again, and that when the

phone rang with my second and third calls he let it ring without answering, because he was fed up with me and with arguing? Or is the truth that she did leave and did come back later but that he remained and let the phone ring without answering? Or did he perhaps bring her in and then go out for the beer while she waited there and listened to the phone ring? The last is the least likely. I don't believe anyway that there was any trip out for beer.

The fact that he does not tell me the truth all the time makes me not sure of his truth at certain times, and then I work to figure out for myself if what he is telling me is the truth or not, and sometimes I can figure out that it's not the truth and sometimes I don't know and never know, and sometimes just because he says it to me over and over again I am convinced it is the truth because I don't believe he would repeat a lie so often. Maybe the truth does not matter, but I want to know it if only so that I can come to some conclusions about such questions as: whether he is angry at me or not; if he is, then how angry; whether he still loves her or not; if he does, then how much; whether he loves me or not; how much; how capable he is of deceiving me in the act and after the act in the telling.

The Fears
of Mrs. Orlando

———

Mrs. Orlando's world is a dark one. In her house she knows what is dangerous: the gas stove, the steep stairs, the slick bathtub, and several kinds of bad wiring. Outside her house she knows some of what is dangerous but not all of it, and is frightened by her own ignorance, and avid for information about crime and disaster.

Though she takes every precaution, no precaution will be enough. She tries to prepare for sudden hunger, for cold, for boredom, and for heavy bleeding. She is never without a bandaid, a safety pin, and a knife. In her car she has, among other things, a length of rope and a whistle, and also a social history of England to read while waiting for her daughters, who are often a long time shopping.

In general she likes to be accompanied by men: they

offer protection both because of their large size and because of their rational outlook on the world. She admires prudence, and respects the man who reserves a table in advance and also the one who hesitates before answering any of her questions. She believes in hiring lawyers and feels most comfortable talking to lawyers because every one of their words is endorsed by the law. But she will ask her daughters or a woman friend to go shopping with her downtown, rather than go alone.

She has been attacked by a man in an elevator, downtown. It was at night, the man was black, and she did not know the neighborhood. She was younger then. She has been molested several times in a crowded bus. In a restaurant once, after an argument, an excited waiter spilled coffee on her hands.

In the city she is afraid of being carried away underground on the wrong subway, but will not ask directions from strangers of a lower class. She walks past many black men who are planning different crimes. Anyone at all may rob her, even another woman.

At home, she talks to her daughters for hours on the telephone and her talk is all premonition of disaster. She does not like to express satisfaction, because she is afraid she will ruin a run of good luck. If she does happen to say that something is going well, then she lowers her voice to say it and after saying it knocks on the telephone table. Her daughters tell her very little, knowing she will find something ominous in what they tell her. And when they tell her so little then she is afraid something is wrong—either their health or their marriage.

One day she tells them a story over the telephone. She has been downtown shopping alone. She leaves the car and goes into a fabric store. She looks at fabrics and does not buy anything, though she takes away a couple of swatches in her purse. On the sidewalk there are many blacks walking around and they make her nervous. She goes to her car. As she takes out her keys, a hand grabs her ankle from under the car. A man has been lying under her car and now he grabs her stockinged ankle with his black hand and tells her in a voice muffled by the car to drop her purse and walk away. She does so, though she can hardly stand. She waits by the wall of a building and watches the purse but it does not move from where it lies on the curb. A few people glance at her. Then she walks to the car, kneels on the sidewalk, and looks under. She can see the sunlight on the road beyond, and some pipes on the belly of her car: no man. She picks up her purse and drives home.

Her daughters don't believe her story. They ask her why a man would do such a peculiar thing, and in broad daylight. They point out that he could not have simply disappeared then, simply vanished into thin air. She is outraged by their disbelief and does not like the way they talk about broad daylight and thin air.

A few days after the assault on her ankle, a second incident upsets her. She has driven her car down at evening to a parking lot beside the beach as she sometimes does, so that she can sit and watch the sunset through her windshield. This evening, however, as she looks over the boardwalk at the water, she does not see the peaceful deserted beach that she usually sees, but a small knot of people standing around something that seems to be lying on the sand.

She is instantly curious, but half inclined to drive away without looking at the sunset or going to see what is on the sand. She tries to think what it could be. It is probably some kind of animal, because people do not stare so long at something unless it has been alive or is alive. She imagines a large fish. It has to be large, because a small fish is not interesting, nor is something like a jellyfish that is also small. She imagines a dolphin, and she imagines a shark. It might also be a seal. Most likely dead already, but it could also be dying and this knot of people intent on watching it die.

Now at last Mrs. Orlando must go and see for herself. She picks up her purse and gets out of her car, locks it behind her, steps over a low concrete wall, and sinks into the sand. Walking slowly, with difficulty, in her high heels through the sand, legs well apart, she holds her hard shiny purse by its strap and it swings wildly back and forth. The sea breeze presses her flowered dress against her thighs and the hem of it flutters gaily around her knees, but her tight silver curls are motionless and she frowns as she plunges on.

She moves in among the people, and looks down. What is lying on the sand is not a fish or a seal but a young man. He is lying perfectly straight with his feet together and his arms by his sides, and he is dead. Someone has covered him with newspapers but the breeze is lifting the sheets of paper and one by one they curl up and slide over the sand to tangle in the legs of the bystanders. Finally a dark-skinned man who looks to Mrs. Orlando like a Mexican puts out his foot and slowly pushes aside the last sheet of newspaper and now everyone has a good look at the dead man. He is handsome and thin, and his color is gray and beginning to yellow in places.

Mrs. Orlando is absorbed in looking. She glances around at the others and she can see they have forgotten themselves too. A drowning. This is a drowning. This may even be a suicide.

She struggles back over the sand. When she gets home, she immediately calls her daughters and tells them what she has seen. She starts by saying she has seen a dead man on the beach, a drowned man, and then she starts over again and tells more. Her daughters are uneasy because she becomes so excited each time she tells the story.

For the next few days, she stays inside her house.

Then she leaves suddenly and goes to a friend's house. She tells this friend that she has received an obscene phone call, and she spends the night there. When she returns home the next day, she thinks someone has broken in, because certain things are missing. Later she finds each thing in an odd place, but she can't lose the feeling that an intruder has been there.

She sits inside her house fearing intruders and watching out for what might go wrong. As she sits, and especially at night, she so often hears strange noises that she is certain there are prowlers below the windowsills. Then she must go out and look at her house from the outside. She circles the house in the dark and sees no prowlers and goes back in. But after sitting inside for half an hour she feels she has to go out again and check the house from the outside.

She goes in and out, and the next day too she goes in and out. Then she stays inside and just talks on the phone, keeping her eyes on the doors and windows and alert to strange shadows, and for some time after this she will not go out except in the early morning to examine the soil for footprints.

Liminal:

The Little Man

———

Lying there trying to sleep, a little light coming through the curtain from the street, she planned things and remembered things and sometimes just listened to sounds and looked at the light and the dark. She thought about the opening and closing of her eyes: that the lids lifted to reveal a scene in all its depth and light and dark that had been there all along unseen by her, nothing to her since she did not see it, and then dropped again and made all that scene unseen again, and could any time lift and show it and any time close and hide it, though often, lying sleepless, her eyes shut, she was so alert, so racing ahead with what she was thinking, that her eyes seemed to her to be wide open behind the closed lids, bugged, glassy, staring, though staring out only into the dark back of the closed lids.

———

Her son came and laid out three large gray shells on her thigh, and the visitor, sitting close to her on another hard chair, reached over to take up the middle one and look at it—an oval cowrie, with white lips.

The moment when a limit is reached, when there is nothing ahead but darkness: something comes in to help that is not real. Another way all this is like madness: a mad person not helped out of his trouble by anything real begins to trust what is not real because it helps him and he needs it because real things continue not to help him.

Her son out on the terrace is dropping a brick over and over again on a plastic gun, breaking it into sharp pieces. The television is on in a room behind a closed door. Another woman comes out with her hair wet and a towel wrapped around her saying suddenly and loudly to him, That's bad, stop it. Her son stands holding the brick, with fear on his face. She says, I was beginning to meditate and I thought the house was falling down. The pieces of red plastic shine on the painted clay around his feet.

How it works: Sometimes there is a thought that becomes a dream (she is laying out a long sentence and then she is out on Fourteenth Street laying out a long piece of black curb) and the mind says, But wait, this isn't true, you're beginning to dream, and she wakes up to think about thinking and dreaming. Sometimes she has lain awake a long time and the stroke of sleep comes down finally and softens every part of her body at once; then her mind notices and wakes because it is interested in how sleep comes so suddenly. Sometimes her mind won't stop working in the first place and won't stop for hours and she gets up to make a warm drink and then it is not the warm drink that helps but the fact that action has been taken. Sometimes sleep comes easily, but almost right away (she has been sleeping ten minutes or so) a loud noise or a soft but offensive noise wakes her and her heart races. First there is only inarticulate anger, then her mind begins working again.

Coughing, her head up on three pillows, warm tea beside her; or on another night a limp, melting rag of wet kleenex across her forehead.

She slept by her son on the beach; they lay parallel to the line of water. The water lapped up in sheets over the sand and drained off. People moved, took positions nearby, walked past, and the sound of the ocean was enough of a silence so that the two slept peacefully, the lowering sun on the boy's face, grains of sand on his neck, an ant running over his cheek (he shuddered, his hand unclenched and then clenched again), her cheek in the soft grayish sand, her glasses and her hat on the sand.

Then there was the slow uphill walk home, and later they went into a dark bar to have dinner (her son nearly asleep bowing over the polished wood) and because of the dark, the crush, the noise, the violent noise, so that they seemed to be swallowing some of all the noise and darkness with their food, she was dizzy and confused when they walked out into the light and the silence of the street.

She is lying in the dark going through some complex turns to get to the point where she can sleep. It is always hard to sleep. Even on nights when it will turn out not to have been hard she expects it to be hard and is ready for it, so that maybe it might as well have been hard.

That night long ago there was nothing more to be done. She lay in a room crying. She lay on her left side with her eyes on the dark window. She was eight or nine, or so. Her left cheek on a soft old pillowcase covering a small old pillow with the smell in it still of old people. Near her, perhaps over against her, under her right arm, her stuffed elephant, nap worn off, trunk creased this way and that. Or more probably tonight, pillow tossed aside, elephant tossed aside, perhaps she has been lying on her right cheek staring at the light that runs under the door and shines on her floorboards, putting a hand down into the draft flowing across the floor; it has been a night of hoping the door will open again, there will be a relenting somewhere, the light will flood in from the hall, white, and against the white light a black figure come in. When the mother is gone at night she is gone very far away, though on the other side of the door, and when she opens the door and comes in, she comes directly to the child and stands at a great height above the child, light on half her face. But tonight the child has not been watching the door, she has her face to the dark window and she has begun crying hopelessly. Someone is angry; she has done some final thing for which there is no forgiveness tonight. No one will come in, and she can't go out. The finality of it terrifies her. It is a feeling close to a feeling she will die of it. Then he comes in, almost of his own accord, though he is not real, she has invented him, he comes in for the first time standing there above her right shoulder, small, soft, self-effacing, something come to tell her she will be all right, come into being at the limit, at the moment when there was nothing ahead but darkness.

She was thinking how it was the unfinished business. This was why she could not sleep. She could not say the day was over. She had no sense that any day was ever over. Everything was still going on. The business not only not finished but maybe not done well enough.

Outside, a mockingbird sang, changing the song often,

every quarter minute or so, as though trying parts of it. She heard him every night, but was not reminded every night but only now and then of a nightingale, which also sings in the dark.

The mockingbird sang, and behind it was the sound of the ocean, sometimes a steady hum, sometimes a sharp clap when a larger wave collapsed on the sand, not every night but when the tide was high at the time when she lay awake in the dark. She thought that if there was a way she could force a kind of peace into herself, then she would sleep, and she tried drawing up this peace into herself, as though it were a kind of fluid, and this worked, though not for long. The peace, when it began to fill her, seemed to come from her spine, the lower part of her spine. But it would not stay in her unless she kept it drawn in there and she could not go on with that for long.

Then she says to herself, Where is there some help in this? And the figure returns, to her surprise, standing above her right shoulder; he is not so small, not so plump, not so modest anymore (years have gone by) but full of a gloomy confidence; he could tell her, though he does not, but his presence tells her, that all is well and she is good, and she has done her best though others may not think so—and these others too are somewhere in the house, in a room somewhere down the hall, standing in a close line, or two lines, with proud, white, and angry faces.

Break It Down

—

He's sitting there staring at a piece of paper in front of him. He's trying to break it down. He says:

I'm breaking it all down. The ticket was $600 and then after that there was more for the hotel and food and so on, for just ten days. Say $80 a day, no, more like $100 a day. And we made love, say, once a day on the average. That's $100 a shot. And each time it lasted maybe two or three hours so that would be anywhere from $33 to $50 an hour, which is expensive.

Though of course that wasn't all that went on, because we were together almost all day long. She would keep looking at me and every time she looked at me it was worth something, and she smiled at me and didn't stop talking and singing, something I said, she would sail into it, a snatch, for me, she would be gone from me a little ways but smiling too, and tell me jokes, and I loved it but didn't exactly know what to do about it and just smiled back at her and felt slow next to her, just not quick enough. So she talked and touched me on the shoulder and the arm, she kept touching and stayed close to me. You're with each other all day long and it keeps happening, the touches and smiles, and it adds up, it builds up, and you know where you'll be that night, you're talking and every now and then you think about it, no, you don't think, you just feel it as a kind of destination, what's coming up after you leave wherever you are all evening, and you're happy about it and you're planning it all, not in your head, really, somewhere inside your body, or all through your body, it's all mounting up and coming together so that when you get in bed you can't help it, it's a real performance, it all pours out, but slowly, you go easy until you can't anymore, or you hold back the whole time, you hold back and touch the edges of everything, you edge around until you have to plunge in and finish it off, and when you're finished, you're too weak to stand but after a while you have to go to the bathroom and you stand, your legs are trembling, you hold on to the door frames, there's a little light coming in through the window, you can see your way in and out, but you can't really see the bed.

So it's not really $100 a shot because it goes on all day, from the start when you wake up and feel her body next to you, and you don't miss a thing, not a thing of what's next to you, her arm, her leg, her shoulder, her face, that good skin, I have felt other good skin, but this skin is just the edge of something else, and you're going to start going, and no matter how much you crawl all over each other it won't be enough, and when your hunger dies down a little then you think how much you love her and that starts you off again, and her face, you look over at her face and can't believe how you got there and how lucky and it's still all a surprise and it never stops, even after it's over, it never stops being a surprise.

It's more like you have a good sixteen or eighteen hours a day of this going on, even when you're not with her it's going on, it's good to be away because it's going to be so good to go back to her, so it's still here, and you can't go off and look at some old street or some old painting without still feeling it in your body and a few things that happened the day before that don't mean much by themselves or wouldn't mean much if you weren't having this thing together, but you can't forget and it's all inside you all the time, so that's more like, say, sixteen into a hundred would be $6 an hour, which isn't too much.

And then it really keeps going on while you're asleep, though you're probably dreaming about something else, a building, maybe, I kept dreaming, every night, almost, about this building, because I would spend a lot of every morning in this old stone building and when I closed my eyes I would see these cool spaces and have this peace inside me, I would see the bricks of the floor and the stone arches and the space, the emptiness between, like a kind of dark frame around what I could see beyond, a garden, and this space was like stone too because of the coolness of it and the gray shadow, that kind of luminous shade, that was glowing with the light of the sun falling beyond the arches, and there was also the great height of the ceiling, all this was in my mind all the time though I didn't know it until I closed my eyes, I'm asleep and I'm not dreaming about her but she's lying next to me and I wake up enough times in the night to remember she's there, and notice, say, once she was lying on her back but now she's curled around me, I look at her closed eyes, I want to kiss her eyelids, I want to feel that soft skin under my lips, but I don't want to disturb her, I don't want to see her frown as though in her sleep she has forgotten who I am and feels just that something is bothering her and so I just look at her and hold on to it all, these times when I'm watching over her sleep and she's next to me and isn't away from me the way she will be later, I want to stay awake all night just to go on feeling that, but I can't, I fall asleep again, though I'm sleeping lightly, still trying to hold on to it.

But it isn't over when it ends, it goes on after it's all over, she's still inside you like a sweet liquor, you are filled with her, everything about her has kind of bled into you, her smell, her voice, the way her body moves, it's all inside you, at least for a while after, then you begin to lose it, and I'm beginning to lose it, you're afraid of how weak you are, that you can't get her all back into you again and now the whole thing is going out of your body and it's more in your mind than your body, the pictures come to you one by one and you look at them, some of them last longer than others, you were together in a very white clean place, a coffeehouse, having breakfast together, and the place is so white that against it you can see her clearly, her blue eyes, her smile, the colors of her clothes, even the print of the newspaper she's reading when she's not looking up at you, the light brown and red and gold of her hair when she's got her head down reading, the brown coffee, the brown rolls, all against that white table and those white plates and silver urns and silver knives and spoons, and against that quiet of the sleepy people in that room sitting alone at their tables with just some chinking and clattering of spoons and cups in saucers and some hushed voices her voice now and then rising and falling. The pictures come to you and you have to hope they won't lose their life too fast and dry up though you know they will and that you'll also forget some of what happened, because already you're turning up little things that you nearly forgot.

We were in bed and she asked me, Do I seem fat to you? and I was surprised because she didn't seem to worry about herself at all in that way and I guess I was reading into it that she did worry about herself so I answered what I was thinking and said stupidly that she had a very beautiful body, that her body was perfect, and I really meant it as an answer, but she said kind of sharply, That's not what I asked, and so I had to try to answer her again, exactly what she had asked.

And once she lay over against me late in the night and she started talking, her breath in my ear, and she just went on and on, and talked faster and faster, she couldn't stop, and I loved it, I just felt that all that life in her was running into me too, I had so little life in me, her life, her fire, was coming into me, in that hot breath in my ear, and I just wanted her to go on talking forever right there next to me, and I would go on living, like that, I would be able to go on living, but without her I don't know.

Then you forget some of it all, maybe most of it all, almost all of it, in the end, and you work hard at remembering everything now so you won't ever forget, but you can kill it too even by thinking about it too much, though you can't help thinking about it nearly all the time.

And then when the pictures start to go you start asking some questions, just little questions, that sit in your mind without any answers, like why did she have the light on when you came in to bed one night, but it was off the next, but she had it on the night after that and she had it off the last night, why, and other questions, little questions that nag at you like that.

And finally the pictures go and these dry little questions just sit there without any answers and you're left with this large heavy pain in you that you try to numb by reading, or you try to ease it by getting out into public places where there will be people around you, but no matter how good you are at pushing that pain away, just when you think you're going to be all right for a while, that you're safe, you're kind of holding it off with all your strength and you're staying in some little bare numb spot of ground, then suddenly it will all come back, you'll hear a noise, maybe it's a cat crying or a baby, or something else like her cry, you hear it and make that connection in a part of you you have no control over and the pain comes back so hard that you're afraid, afraid of how you're falling back into it again and you wonder, no, you're terrified to ask how you're ever going to climb out of it.

And so it's not only every hour of the day while it's happening, but it's really for hours and hours every day after that, for weeks, though less and less, so that you could work out the ratio if you wanted, maybe after six weeks you're only thinking about it an hour or so in the day altogether, a few minutes here and there spread over, or a few minutes here and there and half an hour before you go to sleep, or sometimes it all comes back and you stay awake with it half the night.

So when you add up all that, you've only spent maybe $3 an hour on it.

If you have to figure in the bad times too, I don't know. There weren't any bad times with her, though maybe there was one bad time, when I told her I loved her. I couldn't help it, this was the first time this had happened with her, now I was half falling in love with her or maybe completely if she had let me but she couldn't or I couldn't completely because it was all going to be so short and other things too, and so I told her, and didn't know of any way to tell her first that she didn't have to feel this was a burden, the fact that I loved her, or that she didn't have to feel the same about me, or say the same back, that it was just that I had to tell her, that's all, because it was bursting inside me, and saying it wouldn't even begin to take care of what I was feeling, really I couldn't say anything of what I was feeling because there was so much, words couldn't handle it, and making love only made it worse because then I wanted words badly but they were no good, no good at all, but I told her anyway, I was lying on top of her and her hands were up by her head and my hands were on hers and our fingers were locked and there was a little light on her face from the window but I couldn't really see her and I was afraid to say it but I had to say it because

I wanted her to know, it was the last night, I had to tell
her then or I'd never have another chance, I just said,
Before you go to sleep, I have to tell you before you
go to sleep that I love you, and immediately, right away
after, she said, I love you too, and it sounded to me as
if she didn't mean it, a little flat, but then it usually
sounds a little flat when someone says, I love you too,
because they're just saying it back even if they do mean
it, and the problem is that I'll never know if she meant
it, or maybe someday she'll tell me whether she meant
it or not, but there's no way to know now, and I'm
sorry I did that, it was a trap I didn't mean to put her
in, I can see it was a trap, because if she hadn't said
anything at all I know that would have hurt too, as
though she were taking something from me and just
accepting it and not giving anything back, so she really
had to, even just to be kind to me, she had to say it,
and I don't really know now if she meant it.

Another bad time, or it wasn't exactly bad, but it
wasn't easy either, was when I had to leave, the time
was coming, and I was beginning to tremble and feel
empty, nothing in the middle of me, nothing inside,
and nothing to hold me up on my legs, and then it came,
everything was ready, and I had to go, and so it was
just a kiss, a quick one, as though we were afraid of
what might happen after a kiss, and she was almost wild
then, she reached up to a hook by the door and took an
old shirt, a green and blue shirt from the hook, and put

it in my arms, for me to take away, the soft cloth was full of her smell, and then we stood there close together looking at a piece of paper she had in her hand and I didn't lose any of it, I was holding it tight, that last minute or two, because this was it, we'd come to the end of it, things always change, so this was really it, over.

Maybe it works out all right, maybe you haven't lost for doing it, I don't know, no, really, sometimes when you think of it you feel like a prince really, you feel just like a king, and then other times you're afraid, you're afraid, not all the time but now and then, of what it's going to do to you, and it's hard to know what to do with it now.

Walking away I looked back once and the door was still open, I could see her standing far back in the dark of the room, I could only really see her white face still looking out at me, and her white arms.

I guess you get to a point where you look at that pain as if it were there in front of you three feet away lying in a box, an open box, in a window somewhere. It's hard and cold, like a bar of metal. You just look at it there and say, All right, I'll take it, I'll buy it. That's what it is. Because you know all about it before you even go into this thing. You know the pain is part of the whole thing. And it isn't that you can say afterwards the pleasure was greater than the pain and that's why you would do it again. That has nothing to do with it.

You can't measure it, because the pain comes after and it lasts longer. So the question really is, Why doesn't that pain make you say, I won't do it again? When the pain is so bad that you have to say that, but you don't.

So I'm just thinking about it, how you can go in with $600, more like $1,000, and how you can come out with an old shirt.

Mr. Burdoff's
Visit to Germany

The Undertaking

Mr. Burdoff is lodged in Cologne for the year with a petty clerk and family in order to learn German. The undertaking is ill conceived and ill fated, for he will waste much of his time in introspection and will learn very little German.

The Situation

He writes to an old school friend in America with great enthusiasm about Germany, Cologne, the house he is staying in, and his lofty room with its excellent view out over a construction site to the mountains beyond. But although his situation seems novel to him, it has actually been repeated many times before without spectacular results. To his old school friend, it sounds all too familiar: the house cluttered with knickknacks, the nosy landlady, the clumsy daughters, and the loneliness of his bedroom. The well-meaning language teacher, the tired students, and the strange city streets.

Lassitude

Mr. Burdoff is no sooner established in what he considers a productive routine than he falls into a state of lassitude. He cannot concentrate. He is too nervous to put down his cigarettes, and yet smoking gives him a headache. He cannot read the words of his grammar book and he hardly feels rewarded even when by a tremendous effort he manages to understand one construction.

Liver Dumplings

Mr. Burdoff finds himself thinking about lunch long before it is time to go down to the dining room. He sits by his window smoking. He can already smell the soup. The table in the dining room will be covered by a lace tablecloth but not yet set for lunch.

Mr. Burdoff is gazing out at the construction site in back of the boardinghouse. In a cradle of raw earth three cranes bow and straighten and rotate from side to side. Clusters of tiny workmen far below stand still with their hands in their pockets.

The soup will be thin and clear, with liver dumplings

floating in it, spots of oil on the surface, and specks of parsley under the coil of rising steam. More often than not, the soup will be followed by a thin veal cutlet and the cutlet by a slice of pastry. Now the pastry is baking and Mr. Burdoff can smell it. The sounds he has been hearing, the many different heavy engines of the cranes and bulldozers grinding down below, are muffled by the sound of the vacuum cleaner beyond his door in the hallway. Then the vacuum cleaner moves to another part of the house. At noon the machines down below fall quiet, and a moment later through the sudden silence Mr. Burdoff hears the voice of his landlady, the squeaking of floorboards in the lower hall, and then the festive rattle of cutlery. These are the sounds he has been listening for, and he leaves his room to go down to lunch.

The Class

His language teacher is pleasant and funny, and everyone in the class has a good time. Mr. Burdoff is relieved to see that although his comprehension is poor, he is not the slowest in the class. There are many unison drills out loud, and he joins in with gusto. He takes pleasure in the little stories the class studies so painfully: for example, Karl and Helga go on a sightseeing trip that ends with a mild surprise, and the students appreciate this with waves of laughter.

Hesitation

Mr. Burdoff sits beside a small Hawaiian woman and watches her very red lips as she describes with agony her travels in France. The hesitation of the members of the class as they attempt to speak is charming; a fresh innocence endows them as they expose their weakness.

Mr. Burdoff Falls in Love

Now Mr. Burdoff feels a growing attraction to the Hawaiian woman, who has moved to a seat directly in front of him. During each lesson he stares at her lacquered black ponytail, her narrow shoulders, and the lower edge of her buttocks which delicately protrude through the opening at the back of her chair within inches of his knees. He hungers for a glimpse of her neatly crossed legs, her ballet slipper bobbing as she struggles to answer a question, and her slim hand as it writes, regularly traveling out across the page and then withdrawing again from sight.

He is enchanted by the colors she wears and the objects she carries with her. Every night he lies awake and dreams of helping her out of a serious difficulty. Every dream is the same and stops just short of the first kiss.

His love, however, is more fragile than he knows, and it dies in a moment the day a tall and sumptuous Norwegian woman joins the class.

The Advent of Helen

As she enters the room, swinging her hips around the crowd of silent students, she seems to Mr. Burdoff magnificent and unwieldy. No sooner has she pulled in her hip to accommodate the writing arm of a chair on one side than her low-slung breast on the other side dislodges the chignon of an angry woman from Aix. The students make some effort to shift out of her way, but their chairs are bolted together in threes and they cannot coordinate their efforts. A slow flush crawls up Helen's throat and cheeks.

To Mr. Burdoff's delight, she pushes past his knees and settles in the empty seat next to him. She smiles apologetically at him and at the class in general. A mingling of warm smells drifts from her armpits, her throat, and her hair, and Mr. Burdoff instantly forgets agreements, inflections, and moods, looks up at the teacher and sees only Helen's white eyelashes.

Mr. Burdoff Takes Helen behind a Statue

Helen succumbs to Mr. Burdoff on their very first date, after an evening spent struggling in the wet grass behind a statue of Leopold Mozart. If it is not hard for Mr. Burdoff to lead Helen to the park in the first place, it is more of a problem to roll her damp girdle up around her waist and then to persuade her, after all the heaving and grunting is over, that she has not been seen by an authority figure or a close friend. Once she is easier on that score, her remaining question to Mr. Burdoff is: Does he still respect her?

Mr. Burdoff during Tannhäuser

Much against his own wishes but out of love for Helen, Mr. Burdoff agrees to attend a Wagner opera at the Cologne opera house. During the first act, Mr. Burdoff, accustomed as he is to the clarity of the eighteenth century, becomes short of breath and is afraid he may faint in his hard seat at the top of the hall. Schooled in the strict progressions of Scarlatti, he cannot detect any advance in this music. At what he considers an arbitrary point, the act ends.

When the lights go up, Mr. Burdoff examines Helen's face. A smile hovers around her lips, her forehead and cheeks are damp, and her eyes glow with satiety, as though she has eaten a large meal. Mr. Burdoff, on the other hand, is overcome by melancholy.

During the rest of the performance, Mr. Burdoff's mind wanders. He tries to calculate the seating capacity of the hall, and then studies the dim frescoes on the underside of the dome. From time to time he glances at Helen's strong hand on the arm of her seat but does not dare disturb her by touching it.

Mr. Burdoff and the Nineteenth Century

Late in their affair, by the time Mr. Burdoff has sat through the entire *Ring* cycle and *The Flying Dutchman*, as well as a symphonic poem by Strauss and what seem to him innumerable violin concertos by Bruch, Mr. Burdoff feels that Helen has taken him deep into the nineteenth century, a century he has always carefully avoided. He is surprised by its lushness, its brilliance, and its female sensibility, and still later, as he travels away from Germany on the train, he thinks of the night—important to the progress of their relationship—when he and Helen made love during her menstruation. The radio was broadcasting Schumann's *Manfred*. As Mr. Burdoff climaxed, sticky with Helen's blood, he confusedly sensed that a profound identification existed between Helen's blood, Helen herself, and the nineteenth century.

Summary

Mr. Burdoff comes to Germany. Lives in a rooming house from which he can see construction. Looks forward to lunch. Eats well every day and gains weight. Goes to class, to museums, and to beer gardens. Likes to listen to a string quartet in the open air, his arms on the metal tabletop and gravel under his feet. Daydreams about women. Falls in love with Helen. A difficult and uncomfortable love. Growing familiarity. Helen reveals her love of Wagnerian opera. Mr. Burdoff unfortunately prefers Scarlatti. The Mystery of Helen's Mind.

Helen's child falls ill and she goes home to Norway to nurse him. She is not sure she won't continue her marriage. Mr. Burdoff writes to her at least once every day. Will she be able to return before he leaves for America? The letters she writes back are very brief. Mr. Burdoff criticizes her letters. She writes less frequently and communicates nothing Mr. Burdoff wants to hear. Mr. Burdoff, finished with his course of study, prepares to leave for America. Alone on his way to Paris, he looks out the train window, feels weak, incapable. Helen sits by her sleeping child, gazes toward the bedroom window, thinks of Mr. Burdoff. Is moved to remember earlier lovers, and their cars.

What She Knew

———

People did not know what she knew, that she was not really a woman but a man, often a fat man, but more often, probably, an old man. The fact that she was an old man made it hard for her to be a young woman. It was hard for her to talk to a young man, for instance, though the young man was clearly interested in her. She had to ask herself, Why is this young man flirting with this old man?

The Fish

———

She stands over a fish, thinking about certain irrevocable mistakes she has made today. Now the fish has been cooked, and she is alone with it. The fish is for her—there is no one else in the house. But she has had a troubling day. How can she eat this fish, cooling on a slab of marble? And yet the fish, too, motionless as it is, and dismantled from its bones, and fleeced of its silver skin, has never been so completely alone as it is now: violated in a final manner and regarded with a weary eye by this woman who has made the latest mistake of her day and done this to it.

Mildred and the Oboe

Last night Mildred, my neighbor on the floor below, masturbated with an oboe. The oboe wheezed and squealed in her vagina. Mildred groaned. Later, when I thought she was finished, she started screaming. I lay in bed with a book about India. I could feel her pleasure pass up through the floorboards into my room. Of course there might have been another explanation for what I heard. Perhaps it was not the oboe but the player of the oboe who was penetrating Mildred. Or perhaps Mildred was striking her small nervous dog with something slim and musical, like an oboe.

Mildred who screams lives below me. Three young women from Connecticut live above me. Then there is a lady pianist with two daughters on the parlor floor and some lesbians in the basement. I am a sober person, a mother, and I like to go to bed early—but how can I lead a regular life in this building? It is a circus of vaginas leaping and prancing: thirteen vaginas and only one penis, my little son.

The Mouse

———

First a poet writes a story about a mouse, in moonlight in the snow, how the mouse tries to hide in his shadow, how the mouse climbs up his sleeve and he shakes it down into the snow before he knows what it is that is clinging to his sleeve. His cat is nearby and her shadow is on the snow, and she is after the mouse. A woman is then reading this story in the bath. Half her hair is dry and half of it is floating in the bathwater. She likes the story.

That night she can't sleep and goes into the kitchen to read another book by the same poet. She sits on a stool by the counter. It is late and the night is quiet, though now and then at some distance a train passes and hoots before a crossing. To her surprise, though she knows it lives there, a mouse comes out of a burner from under a pot and sniffs the air. Its feet are like little thorns, its ears are unexpectedly large, one eye is shut and the other open. It nibbles something off the tray of the burner. She moves and it flashes back in, she is still and in a moment it comes out again, and when she moves again it flashes back into the stove like a snapped elastic. At four in the morning, though she is still wide awake, reading and sometimes watching the mouse, the woman closes her book and goes back to bed.

In the morning a man sits in the kitchen on a stool, the same stool, by the counter, and cradles their young cat in his arms, holding her neck in his broad pink hands and rubbing the crown of her head with his thumbs, and behind him the woman stands leaning against his back, her breasts flattened against his shoulder blades, her hands closed over his chest, and they have laid out crusts of bread on the counter for the mouse to smell and are waiting for the mouse to come out, blindly, and for the young cat to get it.

They stay this way wrapped in nearly complete silence, and they are nearly motionless, only the man's gentle thumbs move over the cat's skull and the woman sometimes lays her cheek down against the man's fragrant soft hair and then lifts it again and the cat's eyes are shifting quickly from point to point. A motor starts up in the kitchen, there is the sudden flare of the gas water heater, the swift passage of some cars on the highway below, and then a single voice in the road. But the mouse knows the company that is there and won't come out. The cat is too hungry to keep still and reaches forth one paw and then another and frees herself from the man's light hold and climbs up on the counter to eat the bread herself.

Often, whenever she can get into the house or is let into the house, the cat crouches sleepily on the counter by the stove, her eyes pointed at the burner where the mouse is likely to appear, but she is not more vigilant than that, half asleep, as though she likes just to place herself in this situation, hunting the mouse but perfectly motionless. Really she is keeping the mouse company, the mouse vigilant or sleeping inside the stove, the cat nearby outside. The mouse has had babies, in the stove, and the cat, too, is carrying kittens in her body, and her nipples are beginning to stand out in the downy fur of her belly.

The woman often looks at the cat and sometimes remembers another story.

The woman and her husband lived in the country in a large empty house. The rooms in this house were so large that the furniture sank into the empty spaces. There were no rugs and the curtains were thin, the window-panes cold in the winter, and the daylight and the electric lights at night were cold and white, and lit the bare floor and the bare walls but did not change the darkness of the rooms.

On two sides of the house, beyond the yard, were stands of trees. One woods was deep and thick and climbed away up over a hill. At the bottom of the hill was a marshy pond in the trees where the water had been caught by the railroad embankment. The tracks and ties were gone from the embankment, and the mound of it was overgrown with saplings. The other stand of trees was thin and bordered a meadow, and deer crossed through to sleep in the meadow. In the winter the woman could see their tracks in the snow and follow where they leaped in from the road. When the weather grew cold the mice would start coming into the house from the woods and the meadow, and run through the walls and fight and squeak behind the baseboards. The woman and her husband were not troubled by the mice, except for the little black droppings everywhere, but they had heard that mice would sometimes chew through the wires in the walls and start fires, so they decided to try and get rid of them.

The woman bought some traps at the hardware store, made of bright brassy coils of metal and new raw wood printed with red letters. The man at the hardware store showed her how to set them. It was easy to get hurt because the springs were very strong and tight. The woman had to be the one to set them because she was always the one who did things like that. In the evening before they went to bed, she set one carefully, afraid of snapping her fingers, and put it down in a place where she and he would not be likely to walk on it when they came into the kitchen in the morning forgetting it was there.

They went to bed and the woman stayed awake reading. She would read until the man woke up enough to complain about the light. He was often angry about something and when she read at night it was the light. Later in the night she was still awake and heard the sound like a gunshot of the trap springing but did not go downstairs because the house was cold.

In the morning she went into the kitchen and saw that the trap had flipped over and there was a mouse in it and blood smeared around on the pink linoleum. She thought the mouse was dead, but when she moved the trap with her foot she saw that it was not. It started flipping around on the linoleum with the trap closed on its head. Her husband came in then and neither of them knew what to do about this half-dead mouse. They thought that the best thing would be to kill it with a hammer or some other heavy thing but if one of them was going to do it, it would be her and she did not have the stomach for it. Bending over the mouse she felt sick and agitated with the fear of something dead or nearly dead or mutilated. Both of them were excited and kept staring at it and turning away from it and walking around the room. The day was cloudy with more snow coming and the light in the kitchen was white and cast no shadows.

Finally the woman decided just to throw it outside, get it out of there, and it would die in the cold. She took a dustpan and pushed it under the trap and the mouse and walked quickly with it out the wooden door to the porch and through the porch and out the storm door and down the steps, afraid all the time that it would jump again and slip off the dustpan. She walked down the pitted concrete walk and across the driveway to the edge of the woods and threw the trap and the mouse out onto the frozen crust of snow. She tried to believe the mouse didn't feel much pain and was in shock anyway; certainly a mouse did not feel exactly the way a person would lying with his head closed in a trap, bleeding and freezing to death out there on the white crust of snow. She could not be sure. Then she wondered if there was any animal that might come along and be willing to eat a mouse that was already dead but preserved by the frost.

They did not look for the trap later. In midwinter the man left and the woman lived on in the house alone. Then she moved to the city and the house was rented to a schoolteacher and his wife and a year later sold to a lawyer from the city. The last time the woman walked through it the rooms were still empty and dark, and the furniture set against the bare walls, though it was different furniture, had the same look of defeat under the weight of that emptiness.

The Letter

————

Her lover lies next to her and since she has brought it up he asks her when it ended. She tells him it ended about a year ago and then she can't say any more. He waits and then asks how it ended, and she tells him it ended stormily. He says carefully that he wants to know about it, and everything about her life, but that he doesn't want her to talk about it if she doesn't want to. She turns her face a little away from him so that the lamplight is shining on her closed eyes. She thought she wanted to tell him, but now she can't and she feels tears under her eyelids. She is surprised because this is the second time today that she has cried and she hasn't cried for weeks.

She can't say to herself that it is really over, even though anyone else would say it was over, since he has moved to another city, hasn't been in touch with her in

more than a year, and is married to another woman.
Now and then she has heard news. Someone gets a
letter from him, and the news is that he is nearly out of
his financial troubles and is thinking of starting a magazine. Before that, someone else has news that he lives
downtown with this woman he later marries. They have
no telephone, because they owe the telephone company
so much money. The telephone company, in those days,
calls her from time to time and asks her politely where
he is. A friend tells her he works nights at the docks
packing sea urchins and comes home at four in the morning. Then this same friend tells her how he has offered
something to a lonely woman in exchange for a large
amount of money that makes the woman feel very insulted and unhappy.

Before that, when he still worked nearby, she would
drive over to see him and argue with him at the gas
station, where he read Faulkner in the office under the
fluorescent lights, and he would look up with his eyes
full of wariness when he saw her come in. They would
argue between customers, and when he was filling a car
she would think what she could say next. Later, after
she stopped going there, she would walk through the
town looking for his car. Once, in the rain, a van turned
a corner suddenly at her and she stumbled over her boots
into a ditch and then she saw herself clearly: a woman
in early middle age wearing rubber boots walking in the
dark looking for a white car and now falling into a ditch,

prepared to go on walking and to be satisfied with the sight of the man's car in a parking lot even if the man was somewhere else and with another woman. That night she walked around and around the town for a long time, checking the same places over and over again, thinking that during the fifteen minutes it had taken her to walk from one end of the town to the other he might have driven up to the spot she had left fifteen minutes before, but she did not find the car.

The car is an old white Volvo; it has a beautiful soft shape. She sees other old Volvos nearly every day, and some are tan or cream-colored—close to the color of his—and some are his color, white, but undented and unrusted. The license plates never have a K in them, and the drivers, always in silhouette, are either women or men with glasses or men with heads that are smaller than his.

That spring she was translating a book because it was the only thing she could do. Every time she stopped typing and picked up the dictionary his face floated up between her and the page and the pain settled into her again, and every time she put the dictionary down and went on typing his face and the pain went away. She did a lot of hard work on the translation just to keep the pain away.

Before that, in late March, in a crowded bar, he told her what she was expecting to hear and what she dreaded hearing. Right away she lost her appetite, but he ate very well and ate her dinner too. He did not have the money to pay for the dinner and so she paid. After dinner he said, Maybe in ten years. She said, Maybe in five, but he didn't answer that.

She stops by the post office to pick up a check. She is already late for where she is going, but she needs the money. She sees his handwriting on an envelope in her mailbox. Though it is very familiar to her, or because it is so familiar to her, she doesn't know right away whose handwriting it is. When she realizes whose it is, she swears aloud over and over again walking back to the car. While she is swearing she is also thinking, and she decides that this envelope will have a check in it for some of the money he owes her. He owes her over $300. If he has been embarrassed about the debt, this would explain the year of silence, and if he now has some money to send her, this would explain the fact that now he is breaking the silence. She gets into the car, puts the key in the ignition, and opens the envelope. There is no check in it, and it is not a letter but a poem in French, carefully copied out in his handwriting. The poem ends *compagnon de silence*. Then his name. She doesn't read all of it because she is late meeting some people she doesn't know very well.

She goes on swearing at him until she gets to the highway. She is angry because he has sent her a letter, and because the letter has immediately made her happy, and then her happiness has brought back the pain. And she is angry because nothing can ever make up for the pain. Though of course it is hard to call it a letter, since it is nothing but a poem, the poem is in French, and the poem was composed by someone else. She is also angry because of the kind of poem it is. And she is also angry because even though later she will try to think of ways to answer this, she has seen right away that there is no possible answer to it. She begins to feel dizzy and sick. She drives slowly in the right-hand lane and pinches the skin of her neck hard until the faintness goes away.

All that day she is with other people and she can't look at the letter again. In the evening, when she is alone, she works on a translation, a difficult prose poem. Her lover calls and she tells him how difficult the translation is but not about the letter. After she is finished working, she cleans the house very carefully. Then she takes the letter out of her purse and goes to bed to see what she can make of it now.

She examines first the postmark. The date and the time of day and the city name are very clear. Then she examines her name above the address. He might have hesitated writing her last name, because there is a small ink blot in a curve of one letter. He has addressed it a little wrong and this is not her zip code. She looks at his name, or rather his first initial, the G. very well formed, and his last name next to it. Then his address, and she wonders why he put a return address on the letter. Does he want an answer to this? It is more likely that he is not sure she is still here and if she is not still here he wants his letter to come back to him so that he will know. His zip code is different from the zip code of the postmark. He must have mailed this somewhere out of his neighborhood. Did he also write it away from home? Where?

She opens the envelope and unfolds the paper, which is clean and fresh. Now she notices more exactly what is on this page. The date, May 10, is in the upper-right-hand corner in a smaller, thicker, more cramped hand than the other writing on the page, as though he wrote it at a different time, either before or after the rest. He writes it first, then stops and thinks, his lips tight shut, or looks for the book he will take the poem from— though that is less likely, because he would have it ready in front of him when he sat down to write. Or he thinks after he is done that he will date it. He reads it over, then dates it. Now she notices that he has put her name at the top, with a comma after it, in line with his name below the poem. The date, her name, comma, then the poem, then his name, period. So the poem is the letter.

Having seen all this, she reads the poem more carefully, several times. There is a word she can't decipher. It comes at the end of a line so she looks at the rhyme scheme and the word it should rhyme with is *pures*, pure (pure thoughts), so that the word she can't read is probably *obscures*, dark (dark flowers). Then she can't read another two words at the beginning of the last line of the octet. She looks at the way he has formed other capital letters and sees that this capital must be *L*, and the words must be *La lune*, the moon, the moon that is generous or kind *aux insensés*—to crazed people.

What she had seen first and the only words she could remember as she drove north on the highway were *compagnon de silence*, companion of silence, and some line about holding hands, another about green meadows, *prairies* in French, the moon, and dying on the moss. She hadn't seen what she sees this time, that although they have died, or these two in the poem have died, they then meet again, *nous nous retrouvions*, we found each other again, up above, in something *immense*, somewhere, which must be heaven. They have found each other crying. And so the poem ends, more or less, we found each other crying, dear companion of silence. She examines the word *retrouvions* slowly, to make sure of the handwriting, that the letters really spell out finding each other again. She hangs on these letters with such concentration that for a moment she can feel everything in her, everything in the room too, and in her life up to now, gather behind her eyes as though it all depends on a line of ink slanted the right way and another line as rounded as she hopes it is. If there can be no doubt about *retrouvions*, and there seems to be no doubt, then she can believe that he is still thinking, eight hundred miles from here, that it will be possible ten years from now, or five years, or, since a year has already passed, nine years or four years from now.

But she worries about the dying part of it: it could mean he does not really expect to see her again, since they are dead, after all; or that the time will be so long it will be a lifetime. Or it could be that this poem was the closest thing he could find to a poem that said something about what he was thinking about companions, silence, crying, and the end of things, and is not exactly what he was thinking; or he happened on the poem as he was reading through a book of French poems, was reminded of her for a moment, was moved to send it, and sent it quickly with no clear intention.

She folds up the letter and puts it back in the envelope, lays it on her chest with her hand on top of it, closes her eyes, and after a while, with the light still on, begins to fall asleep. Half dreaming, she thinks that something of his smell may still be in the paper and she wakes up. She takes the paper out of the envelope and unfolds it and breathes deeply the wide white margin at the bottom of the page. Nothing. Then the poem, and she thinks she can smell something there, though she is probably smelling only the ink.

Extracts from a Life

―――

Childhood

I was brought up in the violin factory, and when I had a fight with my brothers and sisters we even used to hit one another with violins.

If you think of something, do it

Plenty of people often think, "I'd like to do this, or that."

The Japanese poet Issa

As a child I was taught to recite the haiku of the Japanese poet Issa, and I have never forgotten them.

Ah, my old home town,
    Dumplings that they used to make,
        Snow in springtime, too.

Grownups

I cannot live without children. But I love grownups too, because I feel a great sympathy for them—"After all, these people too must die."

My meeting with Tolstoy

One day, as usual, I set off for my father's violin factory, where a thousand people were employed. I entered the office, discovered an English typewriter, and started punching the keys.

Just then the chief of the export department came in. "Master Shinichi!"

I lied and said I had merely been touching the keys.

"I see," he replied simply.

Coward, I thought. Why did I dissemble?

I went to a bookstore, filled with severe anger against myself. Fate led me to a copy of Tolstoy's *Diary*. I opened it at random. "To deceive oneself is worse than to deceive others." These harsh words pierced me to the core.

Several years later when, at twenty-three, I went to Germany to study, the book went with me in my pocket.

A little episode

Here follows a little episode of self-praise.

I was then under the strong influence of Tolstoy.

It was in 1919. I received an unexpected letter in early spring inviting me to join an expedition for biological research. The expedition party on board numbered thirty.

At that time I was inseparable from my violin. It had become a part of me.

Our ship circled the islands. While we walked side by side on the beach, we discovered a most unusual patch of moss of reddish-cobalt color growing high up a sheer cliff.

"I very badly wish to have some of that moss," said Professor Emoto, looking up anxiously.

"I will get it for you from here," I boasted, and borrowed a small scoop from a research member.

It turned out to be situated much higher than expected. Heavens! I thought.

I threw the scoop, under the scrutiny of the whole party.

"Oh, wonderful marvelous!" they cried.

As I listened to their applause, I vowed in my heart never again to do such a foolish thing.

I have learned what art really is

Art is not in some far-off place.

Dr. Einstein was my guardian

I took lodgings in the house of a gray-haired widow and her elderly maid. Both the landlady and the maid were hard of hearing so they did not complain no matter how loudly I practiced the violin.

"I shall no longer be able to look after you," said Dr. M., a professor of medicine, "and so I have asked a friend of mine to keep an eye on you." The friend turned out to be Dr. Albert Einstein, who later developed the theory of relativity.

A maestro who performed too well

Einstein's specialties, such as the Bach *Chaconne*, were magnificent. In comparison with his playing, mine, though I tried to play effortlessly and with ease, seemed to me a constant struggle.

"People are all the same, Madame"

At a dinner party, an old woman wondered how it was that a Japanese could play the violin in such a way as to convey what was German about Bruch.

After a brief interval, Dr. Einstein said quietly, "People are all the same, Madame."

I was tremendously moved.

I now felt as though I were under direct orders from Mozart

The whole program that evening was Mozart. And during the Clarinet Quintet, something happened to me that had never happened before: I lost the use of my arms. After the performance I tried to clap. My blood burned within me.

That night I couldn't sleep at all. Mozart had shown me immortal light, and I now felt as though I were under direct orders from Mozart. He expressed his sadness not only with the minor scale but with the major scale as well. Life and death: the inescapable business of nature. Filled with the joy of love, I gave up sadness.

Well done, young man

I was doing what I wanted to do.

Holding his chopsticks in midair, my father looked at me with a sparkle in his eye. "Well done, Shinichi!"

The House Plans

———

The land was pointed out to me from the road, which ran along the side of the hill above it, and right away I wanted to buy it. If the agent had spoken to me of disadvantages, I would not have heard him at that moment. I was numbed by the beauty of what I saw: a long valley of blood-red vineyards, half flooded with late summer rain; in the distance, yellow fields choked with weeds and thistles and behind them a forest covering a hillside; in the middle of the valley, higher than the fields, the ruin of a farmhouse: a mulberry tree grew up through the broken stone of its garden wall, and nearby, the shadow of an ancient pear tree lay across the carpet of brown, rotted fruit on the ground.

Leaning against his car, the agent said, "There is one room left intact. Inside, it is filthy. They have had animals there for years." We walked down to the house.

Dung was thick on the tiles of the floor. I felt the wind through the stones and I saw daylight through the lofty roof. None of this discouraged me. I had the papers drawn up that same day.

I had looked forward for so many years to finding a piece of land and building a house on it that I sometimes felt I had not been brought into the world for any other purpose. Once the desire was born in me, all my energies were bent on satisfying it: the job which I got as soon as I could leave school was tiresome and demoralizing, but it brought me more and more money as my responsibilities grew. In order to spend as little as possible I lived a very uneventful life and resisted making friends or enjoying myself. After many years I had enough money to leave my job and begin looking for land. Real estate agents drove me from one property to another. I saw so many pieces of land that I grew confused and no longer knew just what I was looking for. When at last the valley came into sight below me, I felt I had been relieved of a terrible burden.

While the warmth of summer lay over the land, I was content, living in my majestic and soot-blackened room. I cleaned it up, filled it with furniture, and set up a drawing board in one corner, where I worked on plans for rebuilding the house. Looking up from my work, I would see the sunlight on the olive leaves and be lured outdoors. Walking over the grass by the house, I watched, with the tired, expectant eyes of a man who has lived all his life in the city, magpies running through the thyme and lizards vanishing into the wall. In stormy weather, the cypresses by my window bent before the wind.

Then the autumn chill came down and hunters stalked near my house. The explosion of their rifles filled me with dread. Pipes from a sewage-treatment yard in the next field cracked and let a terrible smell into the air. I built fires in my fireplace and was never warm.

One day my window was darkened by the form of a young hunter. The man was wearing leather and carrying a rifle. After looking at me for a moment, he came to my door and opened it without knocking. He stood in the shadow of the door and stared at me. His eyes were milky blue and his reddish beard hardly concealed his skin. I immediately took him for a half-wit and was terrified. He did nothing: after gazing at what was in the room, he shut the door behind him and went away.

I was filled with rage. As though he were strolling around a zoo, this man had come up to my stony little pen and rudely examined me. I fumed and paced around the room. But I was lonely there, out in the country, and he had awakened my curiosity. By the time a few days had gone by, I was anxious to see him.

He came again, and this time he did not hesitate at the door, but walked in, sat down on a chair, and spoke to me. I did not understand his country accent. He repeated one phrase twice and then a third time and still

I could only guess at his meaning. When I tried to answer him he had the same trouble understanding my city accent. I gave up and offered him a glass of wine. He refused it. In a diffident sort of way he got up from his chair and ventured to inspect my belongings at closer range. Proceeding from my bookcase around the walls, which were covered with framed prints of houses I particularly liked, some in the Place des Vosges and some in the poor quarters behind Montparnasse, he finally arrived at my drawing board, where he stopped short and stood with his finger in the air, waiting for enlightenment. The fact that I was planning a house, line by line, took him a long while to understand and when he did, he began tracing the walls of each room with his finger, a few inches above the blueprint. When at last he had examined and traced every line, he smiled at me without parting his lips, looking sideways in a rather sly way which I did not understand, and abruptly left me.

Again I was angry, feeling that he had invaded my room and stolen my secrets. Yet when my anger subsided I wanted him to return. He returned the following day, and a few days later he came yet again, though the wind was high. I began to expect him and look forward to his visits. He hunted every morning very early, and several times in the week, after he was finished, he would walk in from the field, where the sun was beginning to color the white clay. His face would gleam and he would be so full of energy that he could hardly contain it: leaping up every few minutes from his chair, he would pace to the door and look out, return to the middle of the room, whistling tunelessly, and sit down again. Slowly this energy would die away, and when it was gone, he would go too. He never accepted anything to eat or drink, and seemed surprised that I would offer it, as though sharing food and drink were an act of great intimacy.

It did not become any easier for us to communicate, but we found more and more things to do together. He helped me prepare for winter by filling the chinks in my walls and stacking wood for the fireplace. After we had worked, we would go out into the fields and the forest. My friend showed me the places he liked to visit—a grove of hawthorns, a rabbit warren, and a cave in the hillside—and though I had only one thing that I could show him, he seemed to find it just as mysterious and absorbing as I did.

Each time he came to see me, we would first go over to my blueprint, where I had added another room or increased the size of my study. There were always changes to show him, because I was never done improving my plan and worked on it almost every hour. Sometimes, now, he would pick up my pencil and awkwardly sketch in something that would not have occurred to me: a smokehouse or a root cellar.

But the excitement of the plan as well as the pleasure

of having a friend were blinding me to a dreadful fact: the longer I lived on my land, letting the time slip by, the more the possibility of building the house faded. My money was trickling away and my dream was going with it. In the village, far from any marketplace, the price of food was double what it had been in the city. Thin as I was, I could not eat any less. Good masons and carpenters, even poor ones, were rare and expensive here: to hire a pair of them for a few months would leave me too little to live on afterwards. I did not give up when I learned this, but I had no answers to the questions that plagued me.

In the beginning, my blueprint had absorbed all my time and attention because I was going to build the house from it. Gradually, the blueprint became more vivid to me than the actual house: in my imagination, I spent more and more time among the penciled lines that shifted at my will. Yet if I had openly admitted that there was no longer any possibility of building this house, the blueprint would have lost its meaning. So I continued to believe in the house, while all the time the possibility of building it eroded steadily from under my belief.

What made the situation all the more frustrating was that on the outskirts of the village new houses were springing up every few months. When I had bought the land, the only structures in the valley were stone field huts—squatting in the middle of each plowed field, they were as black as caves inside, with floors of earth. After

signing the deed, I had returned home and stood, well
satisfied, looking across the acres of abandoned vineyards and overgrown farmland to the horizon where the
village sat piled up on a small hill, like a castle, with its
church steeples clustered at the top. Now, here and there
on the landscape, there was a wound of raw red earth
and in a few weeks a new house would rise like a scab
above it. There was no time for the landscape to absorb
these changes: hardly had one house been finished before
the live oaks were felled right and left for another.

I watched the progress of one house with particular
horror and misgiving, because it was within a few minutes' walk of my own. The deliberate speed with which
it went up shook me and seemed a mockery of my own
situation. It was an ugly house, with pink walls and
cheap iron grillwork over the windows. Once it was
finished, and the last young tree planted in the dust
beside it, the owners drove up from the city and spent
All Saints' Day there, sitting on the terrace and looking
out over the valley as though they had box seats at the
opera. After that, as long as the weather held, they drove
up to the house every weekend, filling the countryside
with the noise of their radio. I watched them gloomily
from my window.

The worst of it was that my friend immediately stopped
visiting me on the weekends. I knew he had been drawn
away from me by my neighbors. From a distance I saw
him standing quietly among them in their yard. I felt

utterly miserable. At last I had to admit how bleak my position was. It occurred to me then to sell my land and begin all over again somewhere else.

I thought I might get a good price for the land from other city people. But when I went to see the real estate agent, he told me flatly that because there was a sewage yard in the next field and because my house was un-inhabitable, my property would be almost impossible to sell. He went on to say that the only people who might be interested in buying it were my neighbors, who had in fact resented my presence all this time and would give a very low sum for the land just to be rid of me. They had told the agent in confidence that my house was an eyesore in their front yard and an embarrassment when friends came to spend the day. I was shocked. My strongest feeling, of course, was that I would never sell to my neighbors. I would never give them that triumph. I turned my back on the agent and left without saying a word. As I stood deliberating on the doorstep, I heard him go into another room, say something to his wife, and laugh loudly. This was a very low point in my life.

When, after several weeks, my friend stopped coming altogether, without a word to explain his absence, my bitterness was complete. I sank into a deep depression and decided that I would give up the idea of building a house and return to my job in the city. The directors of my company had not been able to find anyone else will-

ing to put up with the long hours and devote himself
to such interminable complications. They had several
times written asking me to return and offering me more
money. I could easily slip back into my old way of life,
I thought; this stay in the country would then have been
a protracted holiday. I even managed to convince myself, for a moment, that I missed city life and my few
acquaintances in the office, who used to buy me drinks
after particularly tedious days. I told the agent to make
an offer to my neighbors, and tried to think that I was
doing the right thing. But my heart was not in the move,
and I felt like a changed man as I packed up my belongings and took a last walk around my narrow bound-
aries.

The suitcases were out in the early sunlight before the
door of the house, the taxi I had hired was bumping
over the dirt road toward me, and I was really on the
point of leaving, when I thought I might have been too
hasty. It would be wrong to go without saying anything
to the young man who had been my friend, whose name
I did not even know. I paid off the taxi driver and told
him to come at the same hour the following day. He
gave me a doubtful look and drove back down the road.
The dust swirled up behind him and settled. I carried
my suitcases inside and sat down. After I had spent some
time wondering how to find my friend, I realized that
of course I had been foolish, that I had pointlessly com-
mitted myself to one more day in these hostile sur-

roundings, that I would not be able to find him. The directors would be annoyed when I did not arrive at the office, they would worry about me and make an attempt to reach me, and would be completely at a loss when they did not succeed. As the morning advanced I became more and more restless and angry with myself, and felt that I had made a terrible mistake. It was small comfort to know that on the following day everything would go forward as planned, and that in the end it would seem as though this day had never passed at all.

During the long, hot afternoon, small birds fluttered in the thorny brush and a sweet smell rose from the earth. The sky was without clouds and the sun cast black shadows over the ground. I sat in my business suit by the wall of the house and was not touched by the beauty of the land. My thoughts were in the city, and my imprisonment in the country chafed me. At supper time there was nothing to eat, but I was not willing to walk to the village. I lay awake cold and hungry for hours before falling asleep.

I awoke before sunrise. I was so hungry that I felt I had stones in my stomach and I looked forward to eating some breakfast at the train station. Everything outside my window was black. Gusts of wind began moving the leaves as the sky became white behind the black bushes. Color slowly came into the leaves. In the forest and closer to the house bird songs rose and fell on all sides. I listened very intently to them. When the rays of

sunlight reached the bushes I went outside and sat by
the house. When at last the taxi came, I felt so peaceful
that I could not bring myself to leave. After some angry
words, the driver went away.

Throughout the morning and into the afternoon, I sat
in my business suit beside the house, as I had sat the
day before, but I was no longer impatient or eager to
be elsewhere. I was absorbed in watching what passed
before me—birds disappearing into the bushes, bugs
crawling around stones—as though I were invisible, as
though I were watching it all in my own absence. Or,
being where I should not be, where no one expected me
to be, I was a mere shadow of myself, lagging behind
for an instant, caught in the light; soon the strap would
tighten and I would be gone, flying in pursuit of myself:
for the moment, I was at liberty.

When evening came I did not know I was hungry.
Lightheaded with contentment, I continued to sit still,
waiting. Driven inside by the cold and the darkness, I
lay down and had savage dreams.

The next morning, I saw a figure at the far edge of
the nearest field, walking very slowly across. My eyes
felt as if a long emptiness had been filled. Without knowing it, I had been waiting for my friend. But as I watched
him, his hesitation began to seem unnatural and then it
frightened me: he weaved back and forth over the fur-
rows, put his nose up as though sniffing the air like a
spaniel, and did not seem to know where he was going.

I started to meet him and as I drew closer I saw that his
forehead was wrapped in bandages and that the skin of
his face was an awful color of gray. When I came up to
him he was bewildered and stared at me as though I
were a stranger. I took him by the arm and helped him
over the ground. When we reached the house he pushed
me aside and lay down on my bed. He was trembling
with exhaustion. He had lost so much flesh that his
cheeks were like pits and his hands were claws. He had
such fever in his eyes that I thought wildly of going to
the village for a doctor. But after his breath had returned
to him he began speaking quite tranquilly. He explained
something at great length while I sat uncomprehending
by the bed and listened. He made several motions with
his arms and finally I realized he had been in a hunting
accident. During all the weeks that I had been reproach-
ing him so bitterly, he had been lying in a hospital
somewhere.

He continued to talk on and on, and I found it hard
to concentrate on what he said. I became restless and
impatient. After a while I could not bear it any longer.
I got up and paced stiffly back and forth in the room.
At last he stopped speaking and pointed to one corner
of the room, under the window. I did not understand,
because there was nothing there but the window. Then
I saw that he was trying to point to the drawing board,
which had been dismantled, and that he wanted to see
my blueprint. I unpacked it and gave it to him. Still he

was unsatisfied. I found a pencil in my pocket and gave
it to him too. He began drawing on the blueprint. After
a short time he had covered the entire paper, out to its
edges, with complicated forms. Standing over him and
staring, at last I recognized a tower and what might have
been a doorway among the tangle of lines. When he had
filled the page, I gave him more sheets of paper, and he
continued to work. His hand hardly paused, and what
he drew had the complexity of something conceived and
worked over during many solitary days. When he was
too tired to move the pencil any longer, he fell asleep.
I left him there in the early evening and went to the
village for food.

Returning across the fields to my house, I looked at
the red landscape and felt that it was deeply familiar to
me, as though it had been mine long before I found it.
The idea of leaving it seemed to make no sense at all.
Within a few days my rage and disappointment had
ebbed away, and now, as in the beginning, each thing
I looked at seemed only a shell or a husk that would fall
away and reveal a perfect fruit. Though I was tired, my
mind raced forward: I cleared a patch of land by the
house and put up a stable there; I led black-and-white
cows into it, and nervous hens ran underfoot; I planted
a line of cypress trees on the edge of my property, and
it hid my neighbors' house; I pulled down the ruined
walls and with the same stones raised my own manor,
and when it was finished, I looked upon a spectacle that

would excite the envy of everyone who saw it. My dream would be realized as it was first meant to be.

I might have been delirious. It was not likely that things would end that way. But as I stumbled over the field, sinking deep into a furrow with one step and rising to a crest with the next, I was too happy to suspect that at any moment my frustrations and disappointments, like a cloud of locusts, would darken the sky and descend on me again. The evening was serene, the light smooth and soft, the earth paralyzed, and I, far below, the only moving creature.

The Brother-in-Law

———

He was so quiet, so small and thin, that he was hardly there. The brother-in-law. Whose brother-in-law they did not know. Or where he came from, or if he would leave.

They could not guess where he slept at night, though they searched for a depression on the couch or a disorder among the towels. He left no smell behind him.

He did not bleed, he did not cry, he did not sweat. He was dry. Even his urine divorced itself from his penis and entered the toilet almost before it had left him, like a bullet from a gun.

They hardly saw him: if they entered a room, he was gone like a shadow, sliding around the door frame, slipping over the sill. A breath was all they ever heard from him, and even then they could not be sure it hadn't been a small breeze passing over the gravel outside.

He could not pay them. He left money every week,

but by the time they entered the room in their slow, noisy way the money was just a green and silver mist on their grandmother's platter, and by the time they reached out for it, it was no longer there.

But he hardly cost them a penny. They could not even tell if he ate, because he took so little that it was as nothing to them, who were big eaters. He came out from somewhere at night and crept around the kitchen with a sharp razor in his white, fine-boned hand, shaving off slivers of meat, of nuts, of bread, until his plate, paper-thin, felt heavy to him. He filled his cup with milk, but the cup was so small that it held no more than an ounce or two.

He ate without a sound, and cleanly, he let no drop fall from his mouth. Where he wiped his lips on the napkin there was no mark. There was no stain on his plate, there was no crumb on his mat, there was no trace of milk in his cup.

He might have stayed on for years, if one winter had not been too severe for him. But he could not bear the cold, and began to dissipate. For a long time they were not sure if he was still in the house. There was no real way of knowing. But in the first days of spring they cleaned the guest room where, quite rightly, he had slept, and where he was by now no more than a sort of vapor. They shook him out of the mattress, brushed him over the floor, wiped him off the windowpane, and never knew what they had done.

How W. H. Auden
Spends the Night in
a Friend's House:

———

The only one awake, the house quiet, the streets darkened, the cold pressing down through his covers, he is unwilling to disturb his hosts and thus, first, his fetal curl, his search for a warm hollow in the mattress . . .

Then his stealthy excursion over the floor for a chair to stand on and his unsteady reach for the curtains, which he lays over the other coverings on his bed . . .

His satisfaction in the new weight pressing down upon him, then his peaceful sleep . . .

On another occasion this wakeful visitor, cold again and finding no curtain in his room, steals out and takes up the hall carpet for the same purpose, bending and straightening in the dim hallway . . .

How its heaviness is a heavy hand on him and the dust choking his nostrils is nothing to how that carpet stifles his uneasiness . . .

Mothers

———

Everyone has a mother somewhere. There is a mother at dinner with us. She is a small woman with eyeglass lenses so thick they seem black when she turns her head away. Then, the mother of the hostess telephones as we are eating. This causes the hostess to be away from the table longer than one would expect. This mother may possibly be in New York. The mother of a guest is mentioned in conversation: this mother is in Oregon, a state few of us know anything about, though it has happened before that a relative lived there. A choreographer is referred to afterwards, in the car. He is spending the night in town, on his way, in fact, to see his mother, again in another state.

Mothers, when they are guests at dinner, eat well, like children, but seem absent. It is often the case that they cannot follow what we are doing or saying. It is often the case, also, that they enter the conversation only when it turns on our youth; or they accommodate where accommodation is not wanted; smile and are misunderstood. And yet mothers are always seen, always talked to, even if only on holidays. They have suffered for our sakes, and most often in a place where we could not see them.

In a House Besieged

———

In a house besieged lived a man and a woman. From where they cowered in the kitchen the man and woman heard small explosions. "The wind," said the woman. "Hunters," said the man. "The rain," said the woman. "The army," said the man. The woman wanted to go home, but she was already home, there in the middle of the country in a house besieged.

Visit to Her Husband

———

She and her husband are so nervous that throughout their conversation they keep going into the bathroom, closing the door, and using the toilet. Then they come out and light a cigarette. He goes in and urinates and leaves the toilet seat up and she goes in and lowers it and urinates. Toward the end of the afternoon, they stop talking about the divorce and start drinking. He drinks whiskey and she drinks beer. When it is time for her to leave to catch her train he has drunk a lot and goes into the bathroom one last time to urinate and doesn't bother to close the door.

As they are getting ready to go out, she begins to tell him the story of how she met her lover. While she is talking, he discovers that he has lost one of his expensive gloves and he is immediately upset and distracted. He leaves her to look for his glove downstairs. Her story is half finished and he does not find his glove. He is less interested in her story when he comes back into the room without having found his glove. Later when they are walking together on the street he tells her happily how he has bought his girlfriend shoes for eighty dollars because he loves her so much.

When she is alone again, she is so preoccupied by what has taken place during the visit with her husband that she walks through the streets very quickly and bumps into several people in the subway and the train station. She has not even seen them but has come down on them like some natural element so suddenly that they did not have time to avoid her and she was surprised they were there at all. Some of these people look after her and say "Christ!"

In her parents' kitchen later she tries to explain something difficult about the divorce to her father and is angry when he doesn't understand, and then finds at the end of the explanation that she is eating an orange, though she can't remember peeling it or even having decided to eat it.

Cockroaches in Autumn

———

On the white painted bolt of a door that is never opened, a thick line of tiny black grains—the dung of cockroaches.

They nest in the coffee filters, in the woven wicker shelves, and in the crack at the top of a door, where by flashlight you see the forest of moving legs.

Boats were scattered over the water near Dover Harbor at odd angles, like the cockroaches surprised in the kitchen at night before they move.

The youngest are so bright, so spirited, so willing.

He sees the hand coming down and runs the other way. There is too far to go, or he is not fast enough. At the same time we admire such a will to live.

I am alert to small moving things, and spin around toward a floating dust mote. I am alert to darker spots against a lighter background, but these are only the roses on my pillowcase.

A new autumn stillness, in the evening. The windows of the neighborhood are shut. A chill sifts into the room from the panes of glass. Behind a cupboard door, they squat inside a long box eating spaghetti.

The stillness of death. When the small creature does not move away from the lowering hand.

We feel respect for such nimble rascals, such quick movers, such clever thieves.

From inside a white paper bag comes the sound of a creature scratching—one creature, I think. But when I empty the bag, a crowd of them scatter from the heel of rye bread, like rye seeds across the counter, like raisins.

Fat, half grown, with a glossy dark back, he stops short in his headlong rush and tries a few other moves almost simultaneously, a bumper-car jolting in place on the white drainboard.

Here in the crack at the top of the door, moving on their legs, they are in such numbers conscious of us behind our flashlight beam.

It is in his moment of hesitation that you sense him as an intelligent creature. Between his pause and his change of direction, you are sure, there is a quick thought.

They eat, but leave no mark of eating, we think. Yet here in the leaf edge, little crescent shapes—their gradual bites.

He is like a thickened shadow. See how the shadow at the crack of a window thickens, comes out from the wall, and moves off!

In the cardboard trap, five or six of them are stuck— frozen at odd angles, alive with an uncanny stillness, in this box like a child's miniature theater.

How kindly I feel toward another species of insect in the house! Its gauzy wings! Its confusion! Its blundering walk down the lampshade! It doesn't think to run away!

At the end of the meal, the cheeses were brought. All white except the Roquefort, they lay scattered over the board at odd angles, like cows grazing or ships at sea.

After a week, I take a forgotten piece of bread from the oven where they have visited—now it is dry, a bit of brown lace.

The white autumn light in the afternoon. They sleep behind a child's drawings on the kitchen wall. I tap each piece of paper and they burst out from the edges of pictures that are already filled with shooting stars, missiles, machine guns, land mines . . .

The Bone

———

Many years ago, my husband and I were living in Paris and translating art books. Whatever money we made we spent on movies and food. We went mostly to old American movies, which were very popular there, and we ate out a lot of the time because restaurant meals were cheap then and neither of us knew how to cook very well.

One night, though, I cooked some fillets of fish for dinner. These fillets were not supposed to contain bones, and yet there must have been a small bone in one of them because my husband swallowed it and it got caught in his throat. This had never happened to either of us before, though we had always worried about it. I gave him bread to eat, and he drank many glasses of water, but the bone was really stuck, and didn't move.

After several hours in which the pain intensified and my husband and I grew more and more uneasy, we left the apartment and walked out into the dark streets of Paris to look for help. We were first directed to the ground-floor apartment of a nurse who lived not far away, and she then directed us to a hospital. We walked on some way and found the hospital in the rue de Vaugirard. It was old and quite dark, as though it didn't do much business anymore.

Inside, I waited on a folding chair in a wide hallway near the front entrance while my husband sat behind a closed door nearby in the company of several nurses who wanted to help him but could not do more than spray his throat and then stand back and laugh, and he would laugh too, as best he could. I didn't know what they were all laughing about.

Finally a young doctor came and took my husband and me down several long, deserted corridors and around two sides of the dark hospital grounds to an empty wing containing another examining room in which he kept his special instruments. Each instrument had a different angle of curvature but they all ended in some sort of a hook. Under a single pool of light, in the darkened room, he inserted one instrument after another down my husband's throat, working with fierce interest and enthusiasm. Every time he inserted another instrument my husband gagged and waved his hands in the air.

At last the doctor drew out the little fishbone and showed it around proudly. The three of us smiled and congratulated one another.

The doctor took us back down the empty corridors and out under the vaulted entryway that had been built to accommodate horse-drawn carriages. We stood there and talked a little, looking around at the empty streets of the neighborhood, and then we shook hands and my husband and I walked home.

More than ten years have passed since then, and my husband and I have gone our separate ways, but every now and then, when we are together, we remember that young doctor. "A great Jewish doctor," says my husband, who is also Jewish.

A Few Things
Wrong with Me

———

He said there were things about me that he hadn't liked from the very beginning. He didn't say this unkindly. He's not an unkind person, at least not intentionally. He said it because I was trying to get him to explain why he changed his mind about me so suddenly.

I may ask his friends what they think about this, because they know him better than I do. They've known him for more than fifteen years, whereas I've only known him for about ten months. I like them, and they seem to like me, though we don't know each other very well. What I want to do is to have a meal or a drink with at least two of them and talk about him until I begin to get a better picture of him.

It's easy to come to the wrong conclusions about people. I see now that all these past months I kept coming to the wrong conclusions about him. For example, when

I thought he would be unkind to me, he was kind. Then when I thought he would be effusive he was merely polite. When I thought he would be annoyed to hear my voice on the telephone he was pleased. When I thought he would turn against me because I had treated him rather coldly, he was more anxious than ever to be with me and went to great trouble and expense so that we could spend a little time together. Then when I made up my mind that he was the man for me, he suddenly called the whole thing off.

It seemed sudden to me even though for the last month I could feel him drawing away. For instance, he didn't write as often as he had before, and then when we were together he said more unkind things to me than he ever had before. When he left, I knew he was thinking it over. He took a month to think it over, and I knew it was fifty-fifty he would come to the point of saying what he did.

I suppose it seemed sudden because of the hopes I had for him and me by then, and the dreams I had about us—some of the usual dreams about a nice house and nice babies and the two of us together in the house working in the evening while the babies were asleep, and then some other dreams, about how we would travel together, and about how I would learn to play the banjo or the mandolin so that I could play with him, because he has a lovely tenor voice. Now, when I picture myself playing the banjo or the mandolin, the idea seems silly.

The way it all ended was that he called me up on a day he didn't usually call me and said he had finally come to a decision. Then he said that because he had had trouble figuring all this out, he had made some notes about what he was going to say and he asked me if I would mind if he read them. I said I would mind very much. He said he would at least have to look at them now and then as he talked.

Then he talked in a very reasonable way about how bad the chances were for us to be happy together, and about changing over to a friendship now before it was too late. I said he was talking about me as though I were an old tire that might blow out on the highway. He thought that was funny.

We talked about how he had felt about me at various times, and how I had felt about him at various times, and it seemed that these feelings hadn't matched very well. Then, when I wanted to know exactly how he had felt about me from the very beginning, trying to find out, really, what was the most he had ever felt, he made this very plain statement about how there were things about me that he hadn't liked from the very beginning. He wasn't trying to be unkind, but just very clear. I told him I wouldn't ask him what these things were but I knew I would have to go and think about it.

I didn't like hearing there were things about me that bothered him. It was shocking to hear that someone I loved had never liked certain things about me. Of course there were a few things I didn't like about him too, for instance an affectation in his manner involving the introduction of foreign phrases into his conversation, but although I had noticed these things, I had never said it to him in quite this way. But if I try to be logical, I have to think that after all there may be a few things wrong with me. Then the problem is to figure out what these things are.

For several days, after we talked, I tried to think about this, and I came up with some possibilities. Maybe I didn't talk enough. He likes to talk a lot and he likes other people to talk a lot. I'm not very talkative, or at least not in the way he probably likes. I have some good ideas from time to time, but not much information. I can only talk for a long time when it's about something boring. Maybe I talked too much about which foods he should be eating. I worry about the way people eat and tell them what they should eat, which is a tiresome thing to do, something my ex-husband never liked either. Maybe I mentioned my ex-husband too often, so that he thought my ex-husband was still on my mind, which wasn't true. He might have been irritated by the fact that he couldn't kiss me in the street for fear of getting poked in the eye by my glasses—or maybe he didn't even like being with a woman who wore glasses, maybe he didn't like always having to look at my eyes through this blue-tinted glass. Or maybe he doesn't like people who write things on index cards, diet plans on little index cards and plot summaries on big index cards. I don't like it much myself, and I don't do it all the time. It's just a way I have of trying to get my life in order. But he might have come across some of those index cards.

I couldn't think of much else that would have bothered him from the very beginning. Then I decided I would never be able to think of the things about me that bothered him. Whatever I thought of would probably not be the same things. And anyway, I wasn't going to go on trying to identify these things, because even if I knew what they were I wouldn't be able to do anything about them.

Late in the conversation, he tried to tell me how excited he was about his new plan for the summer. Now that he wasn't going to be with me, he thought he would travel down to Venezuela, to visit some friends who were doing anthropological work in the jungle. I told him I didn't want to hear about that.

While we talked on the phone, I was drinking some wine left over from a large party I had given. After we hung up I immediately picked up the phone again and made a series of phone calls, and while I talked, I finished one of the leftover bottles of wine and started on another that was sweeter than the first, and then finished that one too. First I called a few people here in the city, then when it got too late for that I called a few people in California, and when it got too late to go on calling

California I called someone in England who had just woken up and was not in a very good mood.

Between one phone call and the next I would sometimes walk by the window and look up at the moon, which was in its first quarter but remarkably bright, and think of him and then wonder when I would stop thinking of him every time I saw the moon. The reason I thought of him when I saw the moon was that during the five days and four nights he and I were first together, the moon was waxing and then full, the nights were clear, we were in the country, where you notice the sky more, and every night, early or late, we would walk outdoors together, partly to get away from the various members of our families who were in the house and partly just to take pleasure in the meadows and the woods under the moonlight. The dirt road that sloped up away from the house into the woods was full of ruts and rocks, so that we kept stumbling against each other and more tightly into each other's arms. We talked about how nice it would be to bring a bed out into the meadow and lie down on it in the moonlight.

The next time the moon was full, I was back in the city, and I saw it out the window of a new apartment. I thought to myself that a month had passed since he and I were together, and that it had passed very slowly. After that, every time the moon was full, shining on the leafy, tall trees in the back yards here, and on the flat tar roofs, and then on the bare trees and snowy ground in the winter, I would think to myself that another month had passed, sometimes quickly and sometimes slowly. I liked counting the months that way.

He and I always seemed to be counting the time as it passed and waiting for it to pass so that the day would come when we would be together again. That was one reason he said he couldn't go on with it. And maybe he's right, it isn't too late, we will change over to a friendship, and he will talk to me now and then long distance, mostly about his work or my work, and give me good advice or a plan of action when I need one, then call himself something like my *"éminence grise."*

When I stopped making my phone calls, I was too dizzy to go to sleep, because of the wine, so I turned on the television and watched some police dramas, some old situation comedies, and finally a show about unusual people across the country. I turned the set off at five in the morning when the sky was light, and I fell asleep right away.

It's true that by the time the night was over I wasn't worrying anymore about what was wrong with me. At that hour of the morning I can usually get myself out to the end of something like a long dock with water all around where I'm not touched by such worries. But there will always come a time later that day or a day or two after when I ask myself that difficult question once, or over and over again, a useless question, really, since I'm not the one who can answer it and anyone else who tries will come up with a different answer, though of course all the answers together may add up to the right one, if there is such a thing as a right answer to a question like that.

Sketches for

a Life of Wassilly

1

Wassilly was a man of many parts, changeable, fickle, at times ambitious, at times stuporous, at times meditative, at times impatient. Not a man of habit, though he wished to be, tried to cultivate habits, was overjoyed when he found something that truly, for a time, seemed necessary to him and that had possibilities of becoming a habit.

For a while, he sat in his wing chair every evening after supper and found it pleasant. He once thoroughly enjoyed smoking a pipe of fragrant tobacco and thinking over what had happened to him during the day. But the next evening he suffered from wind and could not sit still; the pipe, also, kept going out; the lights for some reason flickered and dimmed constantly, and after a while he gave up the pretense of leisurely contemplation.

Some months later, he decided that a stroll after dinner

was also a popular thing to do and might easily become a habit. For many days he went out of his house at a fixed hour and walked through the neighboring streets, successfully evoking in himself a mood of calm speculation, gazing at the swallows as they flew over the river and at the red sun-soaked housefronts and deducing various ill-founded scientific principles from what he saw; or he let his thoughts dwell on the people that walked by him in the street. But this did not become a habit either: he realized with great disappointment that once he had exhausted all the possible routes within an hour's stroll of his house he became frankly bored with walking, and that instead of benefiting his constitution, it upset his stomach enough so that he had to treat himself with some pills upon returning home. The strolls stopped altogether when his sister came unexpectedly to visit him, and did not resume when she left.

Wassilly was ambitious to learn, and yet sometimes for days on end he could not bring himself to study, but would sneak off into a corner, as if to avoid his own anxious gaze, and spend a long time bent over a crossword puzzle. This made him irritable and dull. He tried to throw the puzzles into a more favorable light by including them in his scheme for self-improvement. During three days, he tested himself against his watch: he did most of a puzzle in twenty minutes on one day, all of it in twenty minutes on the next, and then almost none of it in twenty minutes on the third. On that day he changed the rules and decided he would try to finish the puzzle every day, no matter how long it took. He clearly saw the time coming in which he would be master of the game. To this end he started keeping a notebook in which he wrote down all the more obscure words which appeared regularly in the puzzles and which he otherwise forgot as soon as he learned them, such as "*stoa*: Greek porch." In this way he persuaded himself that he was learning something even from the puzzles, and for a few wonderful hours he saw the conjunction of his baser inclinations and his higher ambitions.

His inconsistency. His inability to finish anything. His sudden terrifying feelings that nothing he did mattered. His realizations that what went on in the outside world had more substance than anything in his life.

Sometimes Wassilly had an inkling that he suffered from a deeper boredom than he could completely picture to himself. At these times, he would brood about the yearly allowance his father gave him: perhaps it was the most unfortunate thing that had ever happened to him; it might ruin what was left of his life. Yet one of the only things Wassilly could be sure of in himself was the recurring hope that things would not turn out as badly as they seemed to be.

His effect on the world was potentially astonishing.

2

Wassilly's few real successes left him unmoved. Or rather, he could not bear to look at an article he had published and would allow his copies of the magazine to become covered with coffee stains and bent at the edges. He could not feel that his printed name was really his, or that the words on the page had really come from his own pen. His sister confirmed this feeling by remaining utterly silent about what he sent to her and also by treating him in exactly the same way she always had—as an agreeable but ineffectual person—when he felt his accomplishments should have made her see him in a new light. As some sort of retaliation, he occasionally wrote her long, deeply serious, and carefully phrased letters criticizing her personal life. These she would only mention months later and in an offhand way.

Not only did his published name and works seem to belong to someone else, but he derived little joy from anything he wrote. Once he had done it, it was out of his hands: it lay in a no-man's-land. It was neutral. It did not speak to him. He wanted to be proud of himself, but felt only guilty—that he had not done more, or better. He envied people who set out to write a book, wrote it, and were pleased with it, and when it was published read it through again with fresh pleasure and turned easily to their next project. He felt only a frightening emptiness ahead of him, a vacancy where there should have been plans, and all his work grew out of impulses.

3

Wassilly was so extremely self-conscious that at times even the soft eyes of his dog made him blush with embarrassment when he tried to attract her attention by some stupid action. Talking to friends on the telephone he would put fantastic interpretations on what they said and respond with clumsy remarks which left them bewildered and nervous.

In strange company he spoke too softly to be heard, afraid that his remarks would be misunderstood. His confidence was further weakened by the fact that people looked puzzled every time he spoke, since they were trying to hear what he was saying, or did not even notice that he had spoken.

Sometimes he was not certain whether or not he should say goodbye to a stranger. He compromised by whispering and looking off to one side.

He did not know exactly when to thank his hostess after attending a dinner or a weekend party. In his uncertainty, he would thank her over and over again. It was as though he did not believe his words carried any weight and hoped to achieve through the effect of accumulation what one speech alone could not accomplish.

Wassilly was puzzled by the fact that these social responses did not come naturally to him, as they evidently did to others. He tried to learn them by watching other people closely, and was to some extent successful. But why was it such a difficult game? Sometimes he felt like a wolf-child who had only recently joined humanity.

4

Wassilly kept falling in love. Even with the dullest and plainest women, since he was so isolated, out there in the country, that his loneliness soon overcame his initial disgust; when he awoke from his madness he would feel disgusted again and embarrassed.

Wassilly had difficult relations with the girl at the grocery. He felt insulted by her cold manner. At home, he sometimes worked himself into a rage against her and made cutting remarks to her out loud. Then he would become ashamed of himself and try to adopt a more enlightened attitude, realizing that she was only an unattractive girl in a small town working in a grocery, someone with no hopes, no ideals, no future. This would restore his sense of proportion. Then he would remember a certain day the previous spring. At the shooting match on a hill above the town she had flaunted herself in a white hat and had not acknowledged his presence by so much as a nod, though all around him people were

in the highest of spirits. As if this was not enough, he
had taken a shot at the target on the next hilltop and the
gun had recoiled and hurt him badly in the shoulder.
Everyone had laughed. But after all, he said to himself,
they were experienced hunters and he was only a fat
intellectual.

5

There were days when nothing went well, in spite of
his good intentions. He would mislay everything he
needed for work—pen, notebook, cigarettes—then after
settling down would be called away to the telephone or
would run out of ink, would resume work and become
suddenly hungry, would be delayed by an accident in
the kitchen and sit down again too distracted to think.

Even after an hour of good work, the day might be
lost: he would feel that a fruitful afternoon was opening
up for him, and on the strength of that feeling would
take a break, stretching his legs in the garden. He would
look up at the sky, his attention would be caught by an
unfamiliar bird, and he would take up his bird book and
follow the bird over the wild acres outside his garden,
plunging through the underbrush, scratching his face,
and gathering burrs on his socks. Returning home, he
would be too hot and tired to work, and with a sense
of guilt would lie down to rest, reading something light.

6

Wassilly sometimes suspected that he worked on his articles only because he enjoyed writing with a fountain pen and black ink. He could not, for example, write anything good with a ballpoint pen. And his work did not go well if he worked with blue ink. When he and his sister played gin rummy together, he enjoyed keeping score—yet if all they had at hand was a pencil, he allowed his sister to keep score.

He liked to use his pen for other things as well: he made lists on scraps of white paper which he saved in a little pile. One list showed what he must remember to do when he visited the city again (Walk in the poorer neighborhoods, Take pictures of certain streets), another what he must do before he left the country (Visit the lake, Take a daylong walk). On another scrap of paper he had written out a tentative schedule for the perfect day, with times set aside for physical exercise, work, serious reading, and correspondence. Then there was a scheme he was outlining for a set of camping equipment which would include a writing table and a cookstove and weigh less than forty pounds. And there were more lists—for example, insoluble problems he was encountering in his study of languages, with suggestions for where to find the answers (and on the list of what he must do in the city he would then add: Visit the library).

But far from helping to organize his life, the lists be-

came very confusing to him. Working on a list, he would
send himself into a certain room to check a book title or
the date and forget why he had gone there, distracted by
the sight of another unfinished project. He received from
himself a number of unrelated instructions which he could
not remember, and spent entire mornings uselessly rush-
ing from room to room. There was a strange gap between volition and action: sitting at his desk, before his
work but not working, he dreamt of perfection in many
things, and this exhilarated him. But when he took one
step toward that perfection, he faltered in the face of its
demands. There were mornings when he woke under a
weight of discouragement so heavy that he could not get
out of bed but lay there all day watching the sunlight move
across the floor and up the wall.

7

Wassilly's conception of himself: Wassilly had been
an exceptionally healthy, agile, and physically fearless
boy—and so he continued to think of himself. Even
when he fell prey to a variety of ailments that followed
one after another with hardly a pause for several years,
he persisted in regarding each ailment as unusual—even
interesting—in a man of his good health. He would not
admit that he was becoming frail, until one day his
sister dropped in to see him where he lay suffering
from a painful sinus attack, and in her blunt way said

that she had never known anyone to get sick so often.

He took up yoga for a time after that, and did a shoulder stand every morning, since according to his book this would "drain one's sinuses and at the same time redistribute one's weight." (There his housekeeper would find him, staring up at a fold of his stomach, his chin pressed into his thyroid.)

He resolved to eat more wisely, taking his protein mainly from yogurt.

Vitamin D, said another book he consulted, was the most difficult vitamin to obtain naturally, and was formed on the oil of the skin by the sun's rays in the hours from ten to two in the months from May to September in Western countries (in the Northern Hemisphere). Accordingly, on the morning of May first, Wassilly exposed most of his skin to the feeble sun, lying for half an hour shivering in his back yard before he could not stand it any longer and gave up. Later, in the summer, he decided to combine the shoulder stand and the sunbath. He went out at noon and pointed his toes at the sky, but becoming dizzy he immediately lost all interest and for a time abandoned both yoga and sunbathing.

The key to everything, he decided, was to relax.

8

Wassilly, suddenly enlightened, saw that there was a terrible discrepancy between his conception of himself and the reality. He admired himself and at times felt slightly superior to others, not because of what he really was and what he had really done with himself, but rather because of what he could do, what he would soon do, what he would accomplish in the years ahead, what he would one day become and remain, and for the courage of his spirit. Sometimes he dreamt of obstacles which he would overcome with glory: fatal illness, permanent blindness, a flood or fire where lives could be saved, a long march as a refugee through mountainous country, a dramatic opportunity to defend his principles. But since under these circumstances it would actually be easier—not more difficult—to perform honorably, it followed that the tedium of his present situation was the most difficult obstacle of all.

One important thing was not to forget what he hoped to achieve in life. Another important thing was not to confuse a romantic picture of himself—as a doctor in Africa, for example—with a real possibility. And he tried not to lose sight of the fact that he was an adult in an adult world, with responsibilities. This was not easy: he would find himself sitting in the sun cutting out paper stars for a Christmas tree at the very moment other men were working to support large families or representing their countries in foreign places. When in moments of difficult truth-seeking he saw this incongruity, he felt sick that he should be saddled with himself, as though he were his own unwanted guest.

9

Wassilly's immobility: In midwinter, Wassilly's brother died. His father asked him to go to the apartment and sort through his brother's things. Wassilly's brother had lived alone in the city. Wassilly had never visited him there, because for some years his brother had not wanted to see him.

The door of the apartment had many locks and Wassilly did not know which were closed and which open, so it took him some time to get inside. Once inside, he was taken aback by the squalor and nakedness of the apartment: it looked like the home of a very poor man. There was nothing on the walls or floors. The furniture was shabby, and there was very little of it.

Wassilly walked through the rooms. Signs of his brother were everywhere. In the bathroom, a web of black fingermarks surrounded the light switch. There was a ring in the tub, and a crust of dirt in the basin and the toilet. In the kitchen glass bottles and jars were crowded into one corner. Sheaths and roots of garlic buds covered the table like a light snow. It was as though his brother would be coming back at any moment.

Wassilly walked into the living room, where the only furniture was a desk, a cupboard, a few chairs, and the unmade bed from which his brother had been taken to the hospital. On the floor under the window, piles of papers and notebooks collapsed out into the room. Wassilly poked through them and found nothing. He pulled a folding wooden chair out into the middle of the room and sat down. He looked out the window at the brick walls of the apartment buildings which abutted this one, enclosing a courtyard and a spindly locust tree.

Wassilly tried to think about his brother—the stooped, thick figure, the slow speech, the hesitations. But again and again his mind wandered. The room was dark, even though the sun shone on the buildings nearby. A neighbor banged something against the wall behind the kitchen stove and immediately afterwards a door slammed in the hallway. Wassilly began to doze off, his chin on his overcoat lapel.

Startled awake by the silence, he looked around the room, so unfamiliar to him. The sun now shone across one wall. Wassilly and his brother had been far apart in age. Wassilly's earliest memories concerned his brother's leaving, returning, and leaving again. Silently he came home, silently left. And Wassilly always at the window, itching with excitement. It was years before Wassilly's admiration withered. By then his brother had no desire to see him anyway.

Wassilly stood up from the folding chair and unbuttoned his overcoat. He had begun to feel slightly nervous. Was this a responsible way to behave? he asked himself. He had come to sort out his brother's things: by now he should have been nearly finished. Yet for an hour he had been sitting in the same position. What would his brother have done in his place? he wondered. His brother would not have come to the apartment at all. He would not even have gone to the funeral.

Wassilly thought of taking off his overcoat but did not. He went into the bathroom, opened the medicine cabinet, and put all the tubes and bottles into a cardboard box for his own use. He felt like a thief. He pulled the towels off the racks and mats off the floor and stuffed them into a large laundry bag. When it came to throwing away his brother's toothbrush, he felt sick and could not go on.

A week later, Wassilly woke up in the right frame of mind, he thought, to do the job. He returned to his brother's apartment. Yet he accomplished no more this time than the last. Something in the very air of the apartment immobilized him. After a few hours he left, carrying away a framed photograph of his grandfather which he had found face down on the mantelpiece. When he got home he wrote to his sister and asked her to do the job for him.

He lay back on his bed that evening, his dog beside him on the floor, and stared over at the photograph of his grandfather, whose eyes twinkled at him out of a dark corner. He could not move, as though the despair of his family life sat on his chest. Layer upon layer of sadness held him down—that he had not seen his brother more, that he had not liked him, that his brother had died alone, that a member of his family should have lived in such squalor. But if his brother had been a stranger, what did the rest matter? Not for the first time, he puzzled over the curious nature of families—that family bonds tended to keep together people who had little in common.

He would never have chosen the members of his family as friends. He thought it was odd that he should have been obliged to go to the apartment of this dirty stranger and handle his things. He looked over at his grandfather's face, with its suppressed smile and carefully folded cravat. He himself had no desire to start a family. Heavily, he rose from his bed and went down to the kitchen. He returned to bed with several thick sandwiches, which he ate until he was too drowsy to keep his eyes open any longer. As he slept and suffered mild nightmares, his dog crept up beside him and wolfed down what remained of the food.

City Employment

———

All over the city there are old black women who have been employed to call up people at seven in the morning and ask in a muffled voice to speak to Lisa. This provides work for them that they can do at home. These women are part of a larger corps of city employees engaged to call wrong numbers. The highest earner of all is an Indian from India who is able to insist that he does not have the wrong number.

Others—mainly old people—have been employed to amuse us by wearing strange hats. They wear them as though they were not responsible for what went on above their eyebrows. Two hats bob along side by side— a Homburg high up on an old man and a black veiled affair with cherries on a little woman—and under the hats the old people argue. Another old woman, bent and feeble, crosses the street slowly in front of our car, looking angry that she has been made to wear this large cone-shaped red hat that is pressing down so heavily on her forehead. Yet another old woman walks on a difficult sidewalk and is cautious about where she sets her feet. She is not wearing a hat, because she has lost her job.

People of all ages are hired by the city to act as lunatics so that the rest of us will feel sane. Some of the lunatics are beggars too, so that we can feel sane and rich at the same time. There are only a limited number of jobs available as lunatics. These jobs have all been filled. For years the lunatics were locked up together in mental hospitals on islands in New York Harbor. Then the city authorities released them in large numbers to form a reassuring presence on the streets.

Naturally some of the lunatics have no trouble holding down two jobs at once by wearing strange hats as they lope and shuffle along.

Two Sisters

———

Though everyone wishes it would not happen, and though it would be far better if it did not happen, it does sometimes happen that a second daughter is born and there are two sisters.

Of course any daughter, crying in the hour of her birth, is only a failure, and is greeted with a heavy heart by her father, since the man wanted sons. He tries again: again it is only a daughter. This is worse, for it is a second daughter; then it is a third, and even a fourth. He is miserable among females. He lives, in despair, with his failures.

The man is lucky who has one son and one daughter, though his risk is great in trying for another son. Most fortunate is the man with sons only, for he can go on, son after son, until the daughter is made, and he will have all the sons he could wish for and a little daughter as well, to grace his table. And if the daughter should never come, then he has a woman already, in his wife the mother of his sons. In himself he has not a man. Only his wife has that man. She could wish for a daughter, having no woman, but her wishes are hardly audible. For she is herself a daughter, though she may have no living parents.

The single daughter, the many brothers' only sister, listens to the voice of her family and is pleased with herself and happy. Her softness against her brothers' brutality, her calm against their destruction, is admired. But when there are two sisters, one is uglier and more clumsy than the other, one is less clever, one is more promiscuous. Even when all the better qualities unite in one sister, as most often happens, she will not be happy, because the other, like a shadow, will follow her success with green eyes.

Two sisters grow up at different times and despise one another for being such children. They quarrel and turn red. And though if there is only one daughter she will remain Angela, two will lose their names, and be stouter as a result.

Two sisters often marry. One finds the husband of the other crude. The other uses her husband as a shield against her sister and her sister's husband, whom she fears for his quick wit. Though the two sisters attempt friendship so that their children will have cousins, they are often estranged.

Their husbands disappoint them. Their sons are failures and spend their mothers' love in cheap towns. Strong as iron, only, is now the hatred of the two sisters for one another. This endures, as their husbands wither, as their sons desert.

Caged together, two sisters contain their fury. Their features are the same.

Two sisters, in black, shop for food together, husbands dead, sons dead in some war; their hatred is so familiar that they are unaware of it. They are sometimes tender with one another, because they forget.

But the faces of the two sisters in death are bitter by long habit.

The Mother

——

The girl wrote a story. "But how much better it would be if you wrote a novel," said her mother. The girl built a dollhouse. "But how much better if it were a real house," her mother said. The girl made a small pillow for her father. "But wouldn't a quilt be more practical," said her mother. The girl dug a small hole in the garden. "But how much better if you dug a large hole," said her mother. The girl dug a large hole and went to sleep in it. "But how much better if you slept forever," said her mother.

Therapy

———

I moved into the city just before Christmas. I was alone, and this was a new thing for me. Where had my husband gone? He was living in a small room across the river, in a district of warehouses.

I moved here from the country, where the pale, slow people all looked on me as a stranger anyway, and where it was not much use trying to talk.

After Christmas snow covered the sidewalks. Then the snow melted. Even so, I found it hard to walk, then for a few days it was easier. My husband moved into my neighborhood so that he could see our son more often.

Here in the city I had no friends either, for a long time. At first, I would only sit in a chair picking hair and dust off my clothes, and then get up and stretch and sit down again. In the morning I drank coffee and smoked. In the evening I drank tea and smoked and went to the window and back and from one room into the next room.

Sometimes, for a moment, I thought I would be able to do something. Then that moment would pass and I would want to move and not be able to move.

In the country, one day, I had not been able to move. First I had dragged myself around the house and then from the porch to the yard, and then into the garage, where finally my brain spun like a fly. There I stood, over an oil slick. I offered myself reasons for leaving the garage, but no reason was good enough.

Night came, the birds quieted down, the cars stopped going by, everything withdrew into the darkness, and then I moved.

All I retrieved from this day was the decision not to tell certain people what had happened to me. I did tell someone, of course, and right away. But he was not interested. He was not very interested in anything about me by then, and certainly not my troubles.

In the city, I thought I might begin to read again. I was tired of embarrassing myself. Then, when I began to read, it was not just one book but many at once—a life of Mozart, a study of the changing sea, and others I can't remember now.

My husband was encouraged by these signs of activity, and he would sit down and talk to me, breathing into my face until I was exhausted. I wanted to hide from him how difficult my life was.

Because I did not immediately forget what I read, I thought my mind was getting stronger. I wrote down facts that struck me as facts I should not forget. I read for six weeks and then I stopped reading.

In the middle of the summer, I lost my courage again. I began to see a doctor. Right away I was not happy with him and I made an appointment with a different doctor, a woman, though I didn't give up the first doctor.

The woman's office was in an expensive street near Gramercy Park. I rang her doorbell. To my surprise, the door was opened not by her but by a man in a bow tie. The man was very angry because I had rung his doorbell.

Now the woman came out of her office and the two doctors began to argue. The man was angry because the woman's patients were always ringing his doorbell. I stood there between them. After that visit I did not go back.

For weeks I did not tell my doctor that I had tried someone else. I thought this might hurt his feelings. I was wrong. In those days it bothered me that he allowed himself to be endlessly abused and insulted as long as I continued to pay his fee. He protested: "I only allow myself to be insulted up to a certain point."

After every session with him, I thought I would not go back. There were several reasons for this. His office was in an old house hidden from the street by other buildings and set in a garden full of little paths and gates and flower beds. Now and then, as I entered or left the house, I glimpsed a strange figure descending the stairs or disappearing through a doorway. He was a short, stout man with a shock of dark hair on his head, tightly buttoned up to the neck in a white shirt. As he passed me he would look at me, but his face revealed nothing, even though I was certainly there, coming up the stairs. This man disturbed me all the more because I did not understand what his relationship with my doctor might be. Halfway through every session I would hear a male voice call one word down the stairway: "Gordon."

Another reason I did not want to continue seeing my doctor was that he did not take notes. I thought he should take notes and remember the facts about my family: that my brother lived by himself in one room in the city, that my sister was a widow with two daughters, that my father was high-strung, demanding, and easily offended, and that my mother criticized me even more than my father. I thought my doctor should study his notes after each session. Instead, he came running down the stairs behind me to make a cup of coffee in the kitchen. I thought this behavior showed a lack of seriousness on his part.

He laughed at certain things I told him, and this outraged me. But when I told him other things that I thought were funny, he did not even smile. He said rude things about my mother, and this made me want to cry for her sake and for the sake of some happy times in my childhood. Worst of all, he often slumped down in his armchair, sighed, and seemed distracted.

Remarkably, every time I told him how uneasy and how unhappy he made me feel, I liked him better. After a few months, I did not have to tell him this anymore.

I thought a very long time went by between visits, and then I would see him again. It was only a week, but many things always happened in a week. For instance, I would have a bad fight with my son one day, my landlady would serve me an eviction notice the next morning, and that afternoon my husband and I would have a long talk full of hopelessness and decide that we could never be reconciled.

I had too little time, now, to say what I wanted to, in each session. I wanted to tell my doctor that I thought my life was funny. I told him about how my landlady tricked me, how my husband had two girlfriends and how these women were jealous of each other but not of me, how my in-laws insulted me over the phone, how my husband's friends ignored me, and then how I kept tripping on the street and walking into walls. Everything I said made me want to laugh. But near the end of the hour I was also telling him how face to face with another person I couldn't speak. There was always a wall. "Is there a wall between you and me now?" he would ask. No, there was no wall there anymore.

My doctor saw me and looked past me. He heard my words and at the same time he heard other words. He took me apart and put me together in another pattern and showed me this. There was what I did, and there was why he thought I did it. The truth was not clear anymore. Because of him, I did not know what my feelings were. A swarm of reasons flew around my head, buzzing. They deafened me, and I was always confused.

Late in the fall I slowed down and stopped speaking, and early in the new year I lost most of my ability to reason. I slowed down still further, until I hardly moved. My doctor listened to the hollow clatter of my footsteps on the stairs and told me he had wondered if I would have the strength to climb all the way up.

In those days I saw only the dark side of everything. I hated rich people and I was disgusted by the poor. The noise of children playing irritated me and the silence of old people made me uneasy. Hating the world, I longed for the protection of money, but I had no money. All around me women shrieked. I dreamed of some peaceful asylum in the country.

I continued to observe the world. I had a pair of eyes, but no longer much understanding, and no longer any speech. Little by little my capacity to feel was going. There was no more excitement in me, and no more love.

Then spring came. I had become so used to the winter that I was surprised to see leaves on the trees.

Because of my doctor, things began to change for me. I was more unassailable. I did not always feel that certain people were going to humiliate me.

I started laughing at funny things again. I would laugh and then I would stop and think: True, all winter I did not laugh. In fact, for a whole year I did not laugh. For a whole year I spoke so quietly that no one understood what I said. Now people I knew seemed less unhappy to hear my voice on the telephone.

I was still afraid, knowing that one wrong move could expose me. But I began to be excited now. I would spend the afternoon alone. I was reading books again and writing down certain facts. After dark, I would go out on the street and stop to look in shop windows, and then I would turn away from the windows, and in my excitement I would bump into the people standing next to me, always other women looking at clothes. Walking again, I would stumble over the curbstone.

I thought that since I was better, my therapy should end soon. I was impatient, and I wondered: How did therapy come to an end? I had other questions too: for instance, How much longer would I continue to need all my strength just to take myself from one day to the next? There was no answer to that one. There would be no end to therapy, either, or I would not be the one who chose to end it.

French Lesson I:

Le Meurtre

———

See the *vaches* ambling up the hill, head to rump, head to rump. Learn what a *vache* is. A *vache* is milked in the morning, and milked again in the evening, twitching her dung-soaked tail, her head in a stanchion. Always start learning your foreign language with the names of farm animals. Remember that one animal is an *animal*, but more than one are *animaux*, ending in *a u x*. Do not pronounce the *x*. These *animaux* live on a *ferme*. There is not much difference between that word, *ferme*, and our own word for the place where wisps of straw cover everything, the barnyard is deep in mud, and a hot dunghill steams by the barn door on a winter morning, so it should be easy to learn. *Ferme*.

We can now introduce the definite articles *le*, *la*, and *les*, which we know already from certain phrases we see in our own country, such as *le car*, *le sandwich*, *le café*, *les girls*. Besides *la vache*, there are other *animaux* on *la ferme*, whose buildings are weather-beaten, pocked with rusty nails, and leaning at odd angles, but which has a new tractor. *Les chiens* cringe in the presence of their master, *le fermier*, and bark at *les chats* as *les chats* slink mewing to the back door, and *les poulets* cluck and scratch and are special pets of *le fermier*'s children until they are beheaded by *le fermier* and plucked by *la femme* of *le fermier* with her red-knuckled hands and then cooked and eaten by the entire *famille*. Until further notice do not pronounce the final consonants of any of the words in your new vocabulary unless they are followed by the letter *e*, and sometimes not even then. The rules and their numerous exceptions will be covered in later lessons.

We will now introduce a piece of language history and then, following it, a language concept.

Agriculture is a pursuit in France, as it is in our own country, but the word is pronounced differently, *agriculture*. The spelling is the same because the word is derived from the Latin. In your lessons you will notice that some French words, such as *la ferme*, are spelled the same way or nearly the same way as the equivalent words in our own language, and in these cases the words in both languages are derived from the same Latin word. Other French words are not at all like our words for the same things. In these cases, the French words are usually derived from the Latin but our words for the same things are not, and have come to us from the Anglo-Saxon, the Danish, and so on. This is a piece of information about language history. There will be more language history in later lessons, because language history is really quite fascinating, as we hope you will agree by the end of the course.

We have just said that we have our own words in English for the same things. This is not strictly true. We can't really say there are several words for the same thing. It is in fact just the opposite—there is only one word for many things, and usually even that word, when it is a noun, is too general. Keep this language concept in mind as you listen to the following example:

A French *arbre* is not the elm or maple shading the main street of our New England towns in the infinitely long, hot and listless, vacant summer of our childhoods, which are themselves different from the childhoods of French children, and if you see a Frenchman standing on a street in a small town in America pointing to an elm or a maple and calling it an *arbre*, you will know this is wrong. An *arbre* is a plane tree in an ancient town square with lopped, stubby branches and patchy, leprous bark standing in a row of similar plane trees across from the town hall, in front of which a bicycle ridden by a man with thick, reddish skin and an old cap wavers past and turns into a narrow lane. Or an *arbre* is one of the dense, scrubby live oaks in the blazing dry hills of Provence, through which a similar figure in a blue cloth

jacket carrying some sort of a net or trap pushes his
way. An *arbre* can also cast a pleasant shade and keep *la
maison* cool in the summer, but remember that *la maison*
is not wood-framed with a widow's walk and a wide
front porch but is laid out on a north-south axis, is built
of irregular, sand-colored blocks of stone, and has a red
tile roof, small square windows with green shutters, and
no windows on the north side, which is also protected
from the wind by a closely planted line of cypresses,
while a pretty mulberry or olive may shade the south.
Not that there are not many different sorts of *maisons* in
France, their architecture depending on their climate or
on the fact that there may be a foreign country nearby,
like Germany, but we cannot really have more than one
image behind a word we say, like *maison*. What do you
see when you say *house*? Do you see more than one kind
of house?

When are we going to return to our *ferme*? As we
pointed out earlier, a language student should master *la
ferme* before he or she moves on to *la ville*, just as we
should all come to the city only in our adolescent years,
when nature, or animal life, is no longer as important
or interesting to us as it once was.

If you stand in a tilled field at the edge of *la ferme*,
you will hear *les vaches* lowing because it is five in the
winter evening and their udders are full. A light is on
in the barn, but outside it is dark and *la femme* of *le
fermier* looks out a little anxiously across the barnyard

from the window of her *cuisine*, where she is peeling vegetables. Now the hired man is silhouetted in the doorway of the barn. *La femme* wonders why he is standing still holding a short object in his right hand. The plural article *les*, spelled *l e s*, as in *les vaches*, is invariable, but do not pronounce the *s*. The singular article is either masculine, *le*, or feminine, *la*, depending on the noun it accompanies, and it must always be learned along with any new noun in your vocabulary, because there is very little else to go by, to tell what in the world of French nouns is masculine and what is feminine. You may try to remember that all countries ending in silent *e* are feminine except for *le Mexique*, or that all the states in the United States of America ending in silent *e* are feminine except for Maine—just as in German the four seasons are masculine and all minerals are masculine—but you will soon forget these rules. One day, however, *la maison* will seem inevitably feminine to you, with its welcoming open doors, its shady rooms, its warm kitchen. *La bicyclette*, a word we are introducing now, will also seem feminine, and can be thought of as a young girl, ribbons fluttering in her spokes as she wobbles down the rutted lane away from the farm. *La bicyclette*. But that was earlier in the afternoon. Now *les vaches* stand at the barnyard gate, lowing and chewing their cuds. The word *cud*, and probably also the word *lowing*, are words you will not have to know in French, since you would almost never have occasion to use them.

Now the hired man swings open *la barrière* and *les vaches* amble across the barnyard, udders swaying, up to their hocks in *la boue*, nodding their heads and switching their tails. Now their hooves clatter across the concrete floor of *la grange* and the hired man swings *la barrière* shut. But where is *le fermier*? And why, in fact, is the chopping block covered with *sang* that is still sticky, even though *le fermier* has not killed *un poulet* in days? You will need to use indefinite articles as well as definite articles with your nouns, and we must repeat that you will make no mistakes with the gender of your nouns if you learn the articles at the same time. *Un* is masculine, *une* is feminine. This being so, what gender is *un poulet*? If you say masculine you are right, though the bird herself may be a young female. After the age of ten months, however, when she should also be stewed rather than broiled, fried, or roasted, she is known as *la poule* and makes a great racket after laying a clutch of eggs in a corner of the poultry yard *la femme* will have trouble finding in the morning, when she will also discover something that does not belong there and that makes her stand still, her apron full of eggs, and gaze off across the fields.

Notice that the words *poule*, *poulet*, and *poultry*, especially when seen on the page, have some resemblance. This is because all three are derived from the same Latin word. This may help you remember the word *poulet*. *Poule*, *poulet*, and *poultry* have no resemblance to the word *chicken*, because *chicken* is derived from the Anglo-Saxon.

In this first lesson we have concentrated on nouns. We can safely, however, introduce a preposition at this point, and before we are through we will also be using one verb, so that by the end of the lesson you will be able to form some simple sentences. Try to learn what this preposition means by the context in which it is used. You will notice that you have been doing this all along with most of the vocabulary introduced. It is a good way to learn a language because it is how children learn their native languages, by associating the sounds they hear with the context in which the sounds are uttered. If the context changed continually, the children would never learn to speak. Also, the so-called meaning of a word is completely determined by the context in which it is spoken, so that in fact we cannot say a meaning is inescapably attached to a word, but that it shifts over time and from context to context. Certainly the so-called meaning of a French word, as I tried to suggest earlier, is not its English equivalent but whatever it refers to in French life. These are modern or contemporary ideas about language, but they are generally accepted. Now the new word we are adding to our vocabulary is the word *dans*, spelled *d a n s*. Remember not to pronounce the last letter, *s*, or, in this case, the next to the last letter, *n*, and speak the word through your nose. *Dans*.

Do you remember *la femme*? Do you remember what

she was doing? It is still dark, *les vaches* are gone from her sight and quieter than they were earlier, except for the one bellowing *vache* who is ill and was not let out that morning by *le fermier* for fear that she would infect the others, and *la femme* is still there, peeling vegetables. She is—now listen carefully—*dans la cuisine*. Do you remember what *la cuisine* is? It is the only place, except perhaps for the sunny front courtyard on a cool late summer afternoon, where *une femme* would reasonably peel *les legumes*.

La femme is holding a small knife *dans* her red-knuckled hand and there are bits of potato skin stuck to her wrist, just as there are feathers stuck in *le sang* on the chopping block outside the back door, smaller feathers, however, than would be expected from *un poulet*. The glistening white peeled *pommes de terre* are *dans une bassine* and *la bassine* is *dans* the sink, and *les vaches* are *dans la grange*, where they should have been an hour ago. Above them the bales of hay are stacked neatly *dans* the loft, and near them is a calf *dans* the calves' pen. The rows of bare light bulbs in the ceiling shine on the clanking stanchions. *Stanchion* is another word you will probably not have to know in French, though it is a nice one to know in English.

Now that you know the words *la femme, dans,* and *la cuisine,* you will have no trouble understanding your first complete sentence in French: *La femme est dans la cuisine.* Say it over until you feel comfortable with it. *La femme est*—spelled *e s t* but don't pronounce the *s* or the *t*— *dans la cuisine*. Here are a few more simple sentences to practice on: *La vache est dans la grange. La pomme de terre est dans la bassine. La bassine est dans* the sink.

The whereabouts of *le fermier* is more of a problem, but in the next lesson we may be able to follow him into *la ville*. Before going on to *la ville*, however, do study the list of additional vocabulary:

> *le sac:* bag
> *la grive:* thrush
> *l'alouette:* lark
> *l'aile:* wing
> *la plume:* feather
> *la hachette:* hatchet
> *le manche:* handle
> *l'anxiété:* anxiety
> *le meurtre:* murder

Once a Very Stupid Man

———

She is tired and a little ill and not thinking very clearly and as she tries to get dressed she keeps asking him where her things are and he very patiently tells her where each thing is—first her pants, then her shirt, then her socks, then her glasses. He suggests to her that she should put her glasses on and she does, but this doesn't seem to help very much. There isn't much light coming into the room. Part of the way through this search and this attempt to dress herself she lies down on the bed mostly dressed while he lies under the covers after earlier getting up to feed the cat, opening the can of food with a noise that puzzled her because it sounded like milk squirting from the teat of a cow into a metal bucket. As she lies there nearly dressed beside him he talks to her steadily about various things, and after a while, as she has been listening to him with different reactions according to what he says to her, first resentment, then great interest, then amusement, then distraction, then resentment again, then amusement again, he asks her if she minds him talking so much and if she wants him to stop or go on. She says it is time for her to get ready to go and she gets up off the bed.

She resumes her search for her clothes and he resumes helping her. She asks him where her ring is and where her shoes are, and where her jacket is and where her purse is. He tells her where each thing is and then gets up and hands her some things even before she asks. By the time she is fully dressed to go, she sees more clearly what is happening, that her situation is very like a Hasidic tale she read on the subway the day before from a book that is still in her purse. She asks him if she can read him a story, he hesitates, and she thinks he probably doesn't like her to read to him, even though he likes to read to her. She says it is only a paragraph, he agrees, and they sit down at the kitchen table. By now he is dressed too, in a white T-shirt and pants that fit him nicely. From the thin brown book she reads the following tale:

"There was once a man who was very stupid. When he got up in the morning it was so hard for him to find his clothes that at night he almost hesitated to go to bed for thinking of the trouble he would have on waking. One evening he took paper and pencil and with great effort, as he undressed, noted down exactly where he put everything he had on. The next morning, well pleased with himself, he took the slip of paper in his hand and read: 'cap'—there it was, he set it on his head; 'pants'—there they lay, he got into them; and so it went until he was fully dressed. But now he was overcome with consternation, and he said to himself: 'This is all very well, I have found my clothes and I am dressed, but where am I myself? Where in the world am I?' And he looked and looked, but it was a vain search; he could not find himself. And that is how it is with us, said the rabbi."

She stops reading. He likes the story, but does not seem to like the ending—"Where am I?"—as much as he likes the beginning, about the man's problem and his solution.

She herself feels she is like the very stupid man, not only because she couldn't find her clothes, not only because sometimes other simple things besides getting dressed are also beyond her, but most of all because she often doesn't know where she is, and particularly concerning this man she doesn't know where she is. She thinks she is probably no place in the life of this man, who is also not only not in his own house, just as she is not in her own house when she visits him and in fact doesn't know where this house is but arrives here as though in a dream, stumbling and falling in the street, but who is not altogether in his own life anymore and might well also ask himself, "Where am I?"

In fact, she wants to call herself a very stupid man.

Can't she say, This woman is a very stupid man, just the way a few weeks before she thought she had called herself a bearded man? Because if the very stupid man in the story behaves just the way she herself would behave or is even right now behaving, can't she consider herself to be a very stupid man, just as a few weeks ago she thought anyone writing at the next table in a café might be considered to be a bearded man? She was sitting in a café and a bearded man was writing two tables away from her and two loud women came in to have lunch and disturbed the bearded man and she wrote down in her notebook that they had disturbed the bearded man writing at the next table and then saw that since she herself, as she wrote this, was writing at the next table, she was probably calling herself a bearded man. It was not that she had changed in any way, but that the words *bearded man* could now apply to her. Or perhaps she had changed.

She has read the tale out loud to him because it is so like what has just happened to her, but then she wonders if it is not the other way around and the tale lodged somewhere in her mind the day before and made it possible for her to forget where all her clothes were and have such trouble dressing. Later that morning, or perhaps on another morning, feeling the same stupidity leaving this man who is not quite in his life anymore, as she looks again for herself in his life and can't find herself anywhere, there are other confusions. She cries and may be crying only because it is raining outdoors and she has been staring at the rain coming down the windowpane, and then wonders if she is crying more because it is raining or if the rain made it possible for her to cry in the first place, since she doesn't cry very often, and finally thinks the two, the rain and the tears, are the same. Then, out on the street, there is a sudden great din coming from several places at once—a few cars honking, a truck's loud engine roaring, another truck with loose parts rattling over an uneven road surface, a roadmender pounding—and the din seems to be occurring right inside her as if her anger and confusion had emptied her and made a place in the middle of her chest for this great clashing of metal, or as if she herself had left this body and left it open to this noise, and then she wonders, Has the noise really come into me, or has something in me gone out into the street to make such a great noise?

The Housemaid

———

I know I am not pretty. My dark hair is cut short and is so thin it hardly hides my skull. I have a hasty and lopsided way of walking, as though I were crippled in one leg. When I bought my glasses I thought they were elegant—the frames are black and shaped like butterfly wings—but now I have learned how unbecoming they are and am stuck with them, since I have no money to buy new ones. My skin is the color of a toad's belly and my lips are narrow. But I am not nearly as ugly as my mother, who is much older. Her face is small and wrinkled and black like a prune, and her teeth wobble in her mouth. I can hardly bear to sit across from her at dinner and I can tell by the look on her face that she feels the same way about me.

For years we have lived together in the basement. She is the cook; I am the housemaid. We are not good servants, but no one can dismiss us because we are still better than most. My mother's dream is that someday she will save enough money to leave me and live in the country. My dream is nearly the same, except that when I am feeling angry and unhappy I look across the table at her clawlike hands and hope that she will choke to death on her food. Then no one would be there to stop me from going into her closet and breaking open her money box. I would put on her dresses and her hats, and open the windows of her room and let the smell out.

Whenever I imagine these things, sitting alone in the kitchen late at night, I am always ill the next day. Then it is my mother herself who nurses me, holding water to my lips and fanning my face with a fly swatter, neglecting her duties in the kitchen, and I struggle to persuade myself that she is not silently gloating over my weakness.

Things have not always been like this. When Mr. Martin lived in the rooms above us, we were happier, though we seldom spoke to one another. I was no prettier than I am now, but I never wore my glasses in his presence and took care to stand up straight and to walk gracefully. I stumbled often, and even fell flat on my face because I could not see where I was going; I ached all night from trying to hold in my round stomach as I walked. But none of this stopped me from trying to be someone Mr. Martin could love. I broke many more things then than I do now, because I could not see where my hand was going when I dusted the parlor vases and sponged the dining-room mirrors. But Mr. Martin hardly noticed. He would start from his fireside chair, as the glass shattered, and stare up at the ceiling in a puzzled sort of way. After a moment, as I held my breath by the glittering pieces, he would pass his white-gloved hand over his forehead and sit down again.

He never spoke a word to me, but then I never heard him speak to anyone. I imagined his voice to be warm and slightly hoarse. Perhaps he stammered when he became emotional. I never saw his face, either, because it was hidden behind a mask. The mask was pale and rubbery. It covered every inch of his head and disappeared beneath his shirt collar. In the beginning it upset me; the first time I saw it, in fact, I lost my head and ran out of the room. Everything about it frightened me—the gaping mouth, the tiny ears like dried apricots, the clumsily painted black hair in frozen waves on its crown, and the naked eye sockets. It was enough to fill anyone's dreams with horror and in the beginning it had me tossing and turning in bed until the sheets nearly choked me.

Little by little I became used to it. I began to imagine what Mr. Martin's real expression was. I saw pink blushes spreading over his gray cheek when I caught him daydreaming over his book. I saw his mouth tremble with emotion—pity and admiration—as he watched me work.

I would give him a certain little look and toss my head, and his face would break into a smile.

But now and then, when I found his pale gray eyes fixed on me, I had the uneasy feeling that I was quite wrong and that perhaps he never responded to me—a silly, inept housemaid; that if one day a different girl were to walk into the room and begin dusting he would only glance up from his book and continue to read without having noticed the change. Shaken by doubt, I would go on sweeping and scouring with numbed hands as though nothing had happened, and soon the doubt would pass.

I took on more and more work for Mr. Martin's sake. Where at first we used to send out his laundry to be washed, I began to wash it myself, even though I did not do it as well. His linen became dingy and his trousers were badly pressed, but he did not complain. My hands became wrinkled and swollen, but I did not mind. Where before a gardener came once a week to trim the hedges in summertime and cover the rosebushes with burlap during the winter, I now took over those duties, dismissing the gardener myself and working day after day in the worst weather. At first the garden suffered, but after a time it came alive again: the roses were driven out by wildflowers of all colors and the gravel walks were disrupted by thick green grass. I grew strong and hardy and didn't mind that my face erupted in welts and the skin of my fingers dried and cracked open, or that with so much work I grew thin and gaunt and smelled like a horse. My mother complained. But I felt that my body was an insignificant sacrifice.

Sometimes I imagined that I was Mr. Martin's daughter, at other times his wife, at other times even his dog. I forgot that I was nothing more than a housemaid.

My mother never once laid eyes on him, and that made my relationship with him all the more mysterious. During the day she stayed below in the steamy kitchen, preparing his meals and chewing her gums nervously. Only in the evening did she step outside the door and stand hugging herself near the overblown lilac bush, looking up at the clouds. Sometimes I wondered how she could go on working for a man she had never seen, but that was her way. I brought her an envelope of money each month and she took it and hid it with the rest of her money. She never asked me what he was like and I never volunteered anything. I think she didn't ask who he was because she hadn't yet even figured out who I was. Perhaps she thought she was cooking for her husband and family like other women, and that I was her younger sister. Sometimes she spoke of going down the mountain, though we don't live on a mountain, or of digging up the potatoes, though there are no potatoes in our garden. This upset me and I would try to bring her out of it by yelling suddenly or baring my teeth in her face. But nothing made any impression, and I would have to wait until at last she called me by name quite naturally. Since she showed no curiosity about Mr. Martin I was left in peace to take care of him just as I wished, to hover about him as he went out of the house on one of his infrequent walks, to linger behind the swinging door of the dining room and watch him through the crack, to brush his smoking jacket and wipe the dust from the soles of his slippers.

But this happiness didn't last forever. I woke up particularly early one Sunday morning in midsummer to see bright sunlight streaming down the hall where I slept. For a long time I lay in bed listening to the wrens that sit and sing in the bushes outside, and watching the swallows that fly in and out of the broken window at the far end of the hallway. I got up and with great care, as always, I cleaned my face and teeth. It was hot. I slipped a freshly washed summer dress over my head and put my feet into my patent leather pumps. For the last time in my life I drowned my own smell in rosewater. Church bells began wildly to chime ten o'clock. When I went upstairs to put his breakfast on the table, Mr. Martin was not there. I waited by his chair for what felt like hours. I began to search the house. Timidly at first, then in a frantic hurry, as though he were slipping out of each room just as I came to it, I looked everywhere for him. Only after seeing that his wardrobe was stripped of his clothes and his bookcase was empty could I admit that he had gone. Even then, and for days afterwards, I thought he might come back.

A week later an old woman came with three or four shabby trunks and began to line the mantelpiece with her cheap knickknacks. Then I saw that without a word of explanation, without regard for my feelings, without even a present of money, Mr. Martin had packed up and gone for good.

This is only a rented house. My mother and I are included in the rent. People come and go, and every few years there is a new tenant. I should have expected that one day Mr. Martin too would leave. But I didn't expect it. I was ill for a long time after that day and my mother, who became more and more loathsome to me, wore herself out bringing me the broth and cold cucumbers that I craved. After my illness I looked like a corpse. My breath stank. My mother would turn away from me in disgust. The tenants shuddered when I came into the room in my clumsy way, tripping over the doorsill even though my glasses again sat like a butterfly on the narrow bridge of my nose.

I was never a good housemaid, but now, though I try hard, I am so careless that some tenants believe I do not clean the rooms at all and others think I am purposely trying to embarrass them in front of their guests. But when they scold me I don't answer. I just look at them indifferently and go on with my work. They have never known such disappointment as I have.

The Cottages

———

1 On the One Hand, On the Other Hand

She is seventy-nine or so, and on the one hand it's
hard to talk to her (she has come for dinner, it's just the
two of us; she eats much more than I thought an old
lady would and even after several helpings of the main
meal and dessert keeps digging into the raisin box with
her knotted fingers and spreading raisins on her clean
plate and nervously lining them up and tossing them
into her mouth as she talks, and when they fall out on
her lower lip tipping them back in), it's hard to talk to
her because she has only four or five things she wants
to talk about and she forgets the name of every person
and the name of every thing she wants to talk about and
when groping to describe the thing whose name she has
forgotten forgets the name of what she needs to describe
to identify to me the first thing she has forgotten (she
closes her eyes, leans her head back, and taps her twisted

fingers on the tablecloth) and in the midst of this de-
scription, because she has gone on trying so long, forgets
why she began it and stops dead or takes a different
direction altogether (she talks with her eyes closed, her
wiry white hair is tied back under a thin piece of yarn,
and then she opens her eyes and cries out at her lolling
dog to lie down and when the dog lies down stamps on
his head in further irritation, and he rolls back his eyes
in fear); on the other hand, even with only four or five
subjects she doesn't exhaust what she has to say because
she entirely forgets that she has made a remark or asked
a question and had an answer to it already, and so she
asks again and I answer again, and she remarks again,
and this happens at intervals all through dinner and beyond (I can't convey the truth to her; there is my truth
and her memory of it; I do not know a friend of hers
but all evening she asks if I know him), but sometimes
she tells me something about the Depression and the
apartments she owned in the city, and then how her
husband wrote his own column for the local paper and
she never knew another writer as fine as he was, and
then that is part of one long story and she remembers
everything that happened and remembers, though she
will have forgotten when I see her again, that she has
told it to me now, though just barely.

2 Lillian

Lillian in her cap of white hair and her ankle socks
and tied brown shoes is a small old woman who works
over her sink before sunrise (I hear it through the wall
of this cottage standing in the trees above the reedy lake
with its black banks of mud and its dock of splintered
wood), who washes her white linen by hand and hangs
it on lines by the cottage and takes it down in the late
morning. Now she sits reading at the picnic table a
picture book about Polish Jews, with her white-framed
glasses directed at the pictures, and when I walk by and
ask, she says she is not really reading but thinking about
sour apples and her daughters, she has been waiting all
day for her two large daughters and waiting also to cook
them the foods of their childhood; but though all day
she is clean and ready, her daughters don't come and
don't call. I look out from time to time and she is still
sitting there alone, and she will not call them for fear
of being a nuisance, and because she is disappointed she
begins to think as she has thought before that she is too
far away, she will not come back to this cottage again
though she has come here for so many years, first with
her husband, then without her husband, who died between one summer and the next, and she is thinking too
how she makes trouble for everyone; well, no one minds!
I have told her, but she will never believe that any more
than she will uncover her old body to swim in company

with the other old people here, and goes down to the lake alone at dawn; and now she puts away her book and her glasses and her shoes untied by the bed, and goes to bed, for it is evening, and she likes to lie and watch the darkness come down into the woods, though tonight, as sometimes before, she does not really watch, or though her eyes rest on the darkening woods, she is not so much watching as waiting, and often, now, feels she is waiting.

Safe Love

—

She was in love with her son's pediatrician. Alone out in the country—could anyone blame her.

There was an element of grand passion in this love. It was also a safe thing. The man was on the other side of a barrier. Between him and her: the child on the examining table, the office itself, the staff, his wife, her husband, his stethoscope, his beard, her breasts, his glasses, her glasses, etc.

Problem

———

X is with Y, but living on money from Z. Y himself supports W, who lives with her child by V. V wants to move to Chicago but his child lives with W in New York. W cannot move because she is having a relationship with U, whose child also lives in New York, though with its mother, T. T takes money from U, W takes money from Y for herself and from V for their child, and X takes money from Z. X and Y have no children together. V sees his child rarely but provides for it. U lives with W's child but does not provide for it.

What an Old Woman
Will Wear

―――

She looked forward to being an old woman and wearing strange clothes. She would wear a shapeless dark brown or black dress of thin material, perhaps with little flowers on it, certainly frayed at the neck and hem and under the arms, and hanging lopsided from her bony shoulders down past her bony hips and knees. She would wear a straw hat with her brown dress in the summer, and then in the cold weather a turban or a helmet and a warm coat of something black and curly like lambswool. Less interesting would be her black shoes with their square heels and her thick stockings gathered around her ankles.

But before she was that old, she would still be a good deal older than she was now, and she also looked forward to being that age, what would be called past the prime of her life and slowing down.

If she had a husband, she would sit out on the lawn

with her husband. She hoped she would have a husband
by then. Or still have one. She had once had a husband,
and she wasn't surprised that she had once had one,
didn't have one now, and hoped to have one later in her
life. Everything seemed to happen in the right order,
generally. She had also had a child; the child was growing, and in a few more years the child would be grown
and she would want to slow down and have someone
to talk to.

She told her friend Mitchell, as they were sitting together on a park bench, that she was looking forward
to her late middle age. That was what she could call it,
since she was now past what another friend had called
her late youth and well into her early middle age. It will
be so much calmer, she said to Mitchell, because of the
absence of sexual desire.

Absence? he said, and he seemed angry, although he
was no older than she.

The lessening of sexual desire, then, she said. He looked
dubious, as far as she could tell, though he was out of
sorts that afternoon and had only looked either dubious
or angry at everything she had said so far.

Then he answered, as though it was one thing he was
sure of, while she was certainly not sure of it, that there
would be more wisdom at that age. But think of the
pain, he went on, or at best the problems with one's
health, and he pointed to a couple in late middle age

who were entering the park together, arm in arm. She had already been watching them.

Right now they are probably in pain, he said. It was true that although they were upright, they held on to each other too firmly and the footsteps of the man were tentative. Who knew what pain they might be suffering? She thought of all the people of late middle age and old age in the city whose pain was not always visible on their faces.

Yes, it was in old age that everything would break down. Her hearing would go. It was already going. She had to cup her hands around her ears in certain situations to distinguish words at all. She would have operations for cataracts on both eyes, and before that she would only be able to see things straight ahead in spots like coins, nothing to the sides. She would misplace things. She hoped she would still have the use of her legs.

She would go into the post office wearing a straw hat that sat too high up on her head. She would finish her business and make her way from the counter out past the line of people waiting that would include a little baby flat on its back in its carriage. She would spot the baby, smile a greedy, painful smile with a few teeth showing, say something out loud to the line of people, who would not respond, and go over to look at the baby.

She would be seventy-six, and she would have to lie down for a while because she had been talking and planned to talk again later in the evening. She was going to a party. She was going to the party only to make sure that certain people knew she was still alive. At the party, nearly everyone would avoid talking to her. No one would admire it when she drank too much.

She would have trouble sleeping, waking often in the night and staying awake early in the morning when it was still dark, feeling as alone in the world as she would ever feel. She would go out early and sometimes dig up a small plant from a neighbor's garden, looking first to see that her neighbor's blinds were down. When she sat in a train or a bus with her eyes fixed on the scenery outside the window, she would hum without stopping for an hour at a time in a high-pitched, quavering voice that sounded a little like a mosquito, so that people around her would become irritated. When she stopped humming, she would be asleep with her head tipped back and her mouth open.

But first there would be the slowing down, a little past the prime, when there would not be as much going on, not as much as there was now, when she wouldn't expect as much, not as much as she did now, when she either would or would not have achieved a certain position which was not likely to change, and best of all when she would have developed some fixed habits, so she would know they were going to sit out on the lawn after supper, for example, she and her husband, and read their books, in the long evenings of summer, her husband in shorts and she in a clean skirt and blouse with her bare feet up on the edge of his chair, and maybe even her mother or his mother there too, reading a book, and the mother would be twenty years older than she was, and therefore well into her old age, though still able to dig in the garden, and they would all dig in the garden together, and pick up leaves, or plan the garden together; they would stand under the sky on this little piece of ground here in the city, planning it out together, the way it should be, surrounding them as they sit in the evening on three folding chairs close together, reading and rarely saying a word.

But she was not only looking forward to that age, she said to Mitchell, when things would slow down and when she would have a husband who had slowed down too, she was also looking forward to a time about twenty years after that when she could wear any hat she wanted to and not care if she looked foolish, and wouldn't even have a husband to tell her she looked foolish.

Her friend Mitchell did not appear to understand her at all.

Though of course she knew it might be true that when the time came, a hat and that freedom would not make up for everything else she had lost with the coming of old age. And now that she had said this out loud, she thought maybe there was no joy, after all, in even thinking about such freedom.

The Sock

—

My husband is married to a different woman now, shorter than I am, about five feet tall, solidly built, and of course he looks taller than he used to and narrower, and his head looks smaller. Next to her I feel bony and awkward and she is too short for me to look her in the eye, though I try to stand or sit at the right angle to do that. I once had a clear idea of the sort of woman he should marry when he married again, but none of his girlfriends was quite what I had in mind and this one least of all.

They came out here last summer for a few weeks to see my son, who is his and mine. There were some touchy moments, but there were also some good times, though of course even the good times were a little uneasy. The two of them seemed to expect a lot of accommodation from me, maybe because she was sick—she was in pain and sulky, with circles under her eyes.

They used my phone and other things in my house. They would walk up slowly from the beach to my house and shower there, and later walk away clean in the evening, with my son between them, hand in hand. I gave a party and they came and danced with each other, impressed my friends, and stayed till the end. I went out of my way for them, mostly because of our boy. I thought we should all get along for his sake. By the end of their visit I was tired.

The night before they went, we had a plan to eat out in a Vietnamese restaurant with his mother. His mother was flying in from another city, and then the three of them were going off together the next day, to the Midwest. His wife's parents were giving them a big wedding party so that all of the people she had grown up with, the stout farmers and their families, could meet him.

When I went into the city that night to where they were staying, I took what they had left in my house that I had found so far: a book, next to the closet door, and somewhere else a sock of his. I drove up to the building and I saw my husband out on the sidewalk flagging me down. He wanted to talk to me before I went inside. He told me his mother was in bad shape and couldn't stay with them, and he asked me if I would please take her home with me later. Without thinking I said I would. I was forgetting the way she would look at the inside of my house and how I would clean the worst of it while she watched.

In the lobby, they were sitting across from each other in two armchairs, these two small women, both beautiful in different ways, both wearing heavy lipstick, different shades, both frail, I thought later, in different ways. The reason they were sitting here was that his mother was afraid to go upstairs. It didn't bother her to fly in an airplane, but she couldn't go up more than one story in an apartment building. It was worse now than it had been. In the old days she could be on the eighth floor if she had to, as long as the windows were tightly shut.

Before we went out to dinner my husband took the book up to the apartment, but he had stuck the sock in his back pocket without thinking when I gave it to him out on the street and it stayed there during the meal in the restaurant, where his mother sat in her black clothes at the end of the table opposite an empty chair, sometimes playing with my son, with his cars, and sometimes asking my husband and then me and then his wife questions about the peppercorns and other strong spices that might be in her food. Then after we all left the restaurant and were standing in the parking lot, he pulled the sock out of his pocket and looked at it, wondering how it had got there.

It was a small thing, but later I couldn't forget the sock, because there was this one sock in his back pocket in a strange neighborhood way out in the eastern part of the city in a Vietnamese ghetto, by the massage parlors, and none of us really knew this city but we were all here together and it was odd, because I still felt as though he and I were partners; we had been partners a long time, and I couldn't help thinking of all the other socks of his I had picked up, stiff with his sweat and threadbare on the sole, in all our life together from place to place, and then of his feet in those socks, how the skin shone through at the ball of the foot and the heel where the weave was worn down; how he would lie reading on his back on the bed with his feet crossed at the ankles so that his toes pointed at different corners of the room; how he would then turn on his side with his feet together like two halves of a fruit; how, still reading, he would reach down and pull off his socks and drop them in little balls on the floor and reach down again and pick at his toes while he read; sometimes he shared with me what he was reading and thinking, and sometimes he didn't know whether I was there in the room or somewhere else.

I couldn't forget it later, even though after they were gone I found a few other things they had left, or rather his wife had left them in the pocket of a jacket of mine— a red comb, a red lipstick, and a bottle of pills. For a while these things sat around in a little group of three on one counter of the kitchen and then another, while I thought I'd send them to her, because I thought maybe the medicine was important, but I kept forgetting to ask, until finally I put them away in a drawer to give her when they came out again, because by then it wasn't going to be long, and it made me tired all over again just to think of it.

Five Signs

of Disturbance

———

Back in the city, she is alone most of the time. It is a large apartment that is not hers, though it is not unfamiliar either.

She spends the days by herself trying to work and sometimes looking up from her work to worry about how she will find a place to live, because she can't stay in this apartment beyond the end of the summer. Then, in the late afternoon, she begins to think she should call someone.

She is watching everything very closely: herself, this apartment, what is outside the windows, and the weather.

There is a day of thunderstorms, with dark yellow and green light in the street, and black light in the alley. She looks into the alley and sees foam running over the concrete, washed out from the gutters by the rain. Then there is a day of high wind.

Now she stands by the door watching the doorknob. The brass doorknob is moving by itself, very slightly, turning back and forth, then jiggling. She is startled, then she hears a foot shuffle on the other side of the doorsill, and a cloth brush against the panel, and other soft noises, and realizes after a moment that this is the doorman who has come to clean the outside of the door. But she does not go away until the doorknob stops moving.

She looks at the clock often and is aware of exactly what time it is now, and then ten minutes from now, even though she has no need to know what time it is. She also knows exactly how she is feeling, uneasy now, angry ten minutes from now. She is sick to death of knowing what she is feeling, but she can't stop, as though if she stops watching for longer than a moment, she will disappear (wander off).

There is a bright light coming from the kitchen. She did not turn a light on there. The light is coming from the open window (it is late summer). It is morning.

On another day, the early, low sun shines on the park across the street, on the near edge of it, so that one bare trunk, and the outer leaves of the trees on this side of the grove, are whitened with sunlight as though someone has thrown a handful of gray dust over them. Behind them, darkness.

Before her as she stands at the front window looking

out at the park, the plants on the windowsill have dropped some of their leaves.

She knows that if she speaks on the telephone, her voice will communicate something no one will want to listen to. And she will have trouble making herself heard.

In the midst of the random noises from the courtyard (she catalogues them in the evening: the clatter of dishes, an electric guitar, a woman's laughter, a toilet flushing, a television, running water), suddenly a quarrel begins, between a man and his mother (he shouts in his deep voice, "Mother!").

She thinks, having come back after some years, that this is a place full of difficulty.

She watches a great deal of television, even though there is very little that she likes and she also has trouble focusing the picture. She watches anything that comes in clearly, even though she may find it offensive. One evening she watches one face in a movie for two hours and feels that her own face has changed. Then, the next night at the same hour, she is not watching television and she thinks: The hour may be the same but the night is not the same.

Later, when she lists and counts the signs of disturbance, at least two are associated with the television.

Now she can't put it off any longer. She has to go out and look for a place to live. She doesn't want to do this, because she doesn't want to say to herself that she really has no place of her own. She would rather do nothing about the problem and stay inside this apartment all day.

Several times she goes out to look at apartments. She can't afford to pay much, and so she looks at the very cheapest apartments. She looks at one above a candy store and one above an Italian men's social club. The third one she looks at is nothing but a shell with a large hole in the floor of the back room, and the garden is overgrown with brambles. The real-estate agent apologizes to her.

She is glad when it grows too late in the afternoon to look at anything more and she can go back to the apartment and watch television and eat and drink.

She often cries over what she sees on television. Usually it is something on the evening news, a death or many deaths somewhere, or an act of heroism, or a film of a newborn baby with a disease. But sometimes an ad, if it involves old people or children, will also make her cry. The younger the child is, the more easily she cries, but even a film of an adolescent will sometimes make her cry, though she does not like adolescents. Often, after the news is over, she is still catching her breath as she walks out to the kitchen.

She eats dinner in front of the television. After another hour or two she begins drinking. She drinks until she is drunk enough so that she drops things and her handwriting becomes hard to read and she leaves out some of the letters from certain words and has to read all the words over again carefully, adding the missing letters and after that printing some words a second time above the illegible script.

She is forgetting the idea she had about moderation.

She does the dishes so wildly that soap flies everywhere and water splashes on the floor and the front of her clothes. During the day she washes her hands often, rubbing them together briskly, almost violently, because she feels that everything she touches is coated with grease.

She stands by the door and hears someone whistling in the marble lobby.

One day she sees an apartment she is willing to take. It is not very pretty, but she is ready to take it because she wants to have a home again, she wants to be bound to this city by a lease, she doesn't want to go on feeling the way she does, loose in the world, the only one without any place. She imagines that when she moves in, she will have a party. She signs some papers. The agent will call her later and tell her whether the deal has gone through or not. She walks home and shops for food with a sort of forced tranquillity, as though if she moves too quickly something will break. She continues to move this way, gently, with deliberation, the rest of the day. Then, later in the evening, the agent calls and tells her she has lost the apartment. The owner has decided suddenly not to rent it. She can hardly believe this explanation.

Now she is sure she will never find a place to live.

She lies in bed with a bottle of beer. She finishes the beer and wants to put it down. She can't put it on the bare wood of the bedside table because it will leave a mark, and the table is not hers. She puts it on a book, but the book is not hers either. She moves it to another book, which is hers, a song book.

Then she gets up because she sees that the clothes she took off earlier are heaped on a chair. She wants to lay them out straight in case she decides to wear them the next day, and she lays them out, but since she is quite drunk they are not straight, as she can see. She is drunk because she has had two bottles of beer, a glass of Drambuie, and then a third bottle of beer.

In spite of being drunk, she can still hold on to some things in her mind, though with an effort. She sees how well she is holding on to things and thinks that she is still smart. She thinks about how her smartness doesn't seem to count for much anymore, the way it used to. Her smartness has counted for less and less as she has grown older. She lies there in the dark trying to pull herself together. She can feel this is a cliff edge, this return. Now it is after two in the morning, but she can't let herself fall asleep.

On the white side of a truck, a dark blue eagle with its wings raised. Watching for it, she sees, outside the window, the mail truck pull up by the hydrant. She sees the mailbag tossed out of the truck onto the sidewalk and the handyman of the building drag it across the sidewalk and then stand holding it by the neck while he talks to another handyman and she grows angry as she watches because there may be a letter for her in the bag.

She is told about an apartment in a nice small street, but she won't look at it because she is also told that on the floor below lives a retarded man and his father and they argue and shout and she would have to listen to that.

The day is dark again with the threat of rain. In the yellow light she sweeps up the dead leaves of the house-plants and waters the pots. On this day there is more order.

In the dining room she pushes upright the heavy books that have been leaning far over to one side on the shelves and sprawling open for so long now that their covers are warped out of shape. There is another bookcase in the living room, with glass doors, and on top of it a clock that hisses every time the second hand passes a certain point. Now she walks down the hall, straightening more books as she comes to them. The hall is long and dark, with many angles, so that around every bend more hallway opens out and this hallway seems to her, sometimes, infinitely long.

In the bedroom, where she watches television, she can often hear the sound of a string quartet or some other classical music. It is a small sound, but perfectly clear. When she first heard it, she wondered if there was a radio somewhere in the room, turned very low. She walked slowly around the room, listening. The walls of the room are dark, the windows are shaded, and there is a large low bureau of scratched green wood with a mirror above it into which she looks again and again, as she also looks into the three long mirrors on the three doors of the closet. The music was coming from the radiator, which stands below a framed photograph of a bearded man; he is the classicist whose books were falling over in the other room. She put her ear down near the radiator and found that the music was coming from the knob. Now she sometimes lies on the bed listening to the music. It is just low enough so that it doesn't stop her from thinking.

One day a fly walks over her hand and she feels that the fly is a friendly presence. The same day, she wants to stop a policeman in the street and talk to him. Then that impulse passes.

She decides to call several people. She tells herself she has to talk to some people. She is worried, and then she is angry at herself for worrying, for always thinking about herself and for always looking at the world so darkly. But she doesn't know how to stop.

She reads a book about Zen and she writes down on

a piece of paper the eight parts of Buddha's eight-fold path and thinks she might follow it. She sees that it mainly involves doing everything right.

Even though it is late enough to go to sleep she has something more to eat. Cereal, then, after the cereal, bread and butter, then marshmallows and other foods. She turns over onto her stomach and looks at the covers of some books. She can go on reading now without eating. Her stomach is so full that she can't lie on it comfortably, and she feels as though she were lying on a rock or a bundle of sticks. She has filled her stomach as though she were filling a knapsack or a boat for a long journey. It will be slow and hot, and she will wake and sleep again several times and have uncomfortable dreams, or there will be no sleep but hard questions. No tears, though.

The rain continues to fall steadily just beyond the sound of an air conditioner. It is a soft drumming with an occasional louder splat into the courtyard.

She can't fall asleep. She lies with her ear on the mattress and listens to her loud heartbeat, first the rush of blood from her heart, which she can feel, then a split second later the thump in her ear. The sound is *shethump, shethump*. Then she starts to fall asleep and wakes again when she begins dreaming that her heart is a police station.

Another night it is her lungs; she shuts her eyes and her lungs seem as large as the room, and as dark, and enclosed in a fragile shell of bone, and in one dark lung she is crouching and the wind whistles around her, in and out.

Some things in her behavior now strike her as odd. Then something happens that should frighten her, but she is not frightened.

The way it happens: at the end of the day she turns on the news and immediately she is addressed eye to eye, with almost unbearable intensity, by a male newscaster. He is the first person who has spoken to her all day. Shaken by these few minutes of direct address, she goes out to the kitchen to make an omelette. She mixes the eggs and pours them into the pan, where the butter is beginning to burn. As the omelette forms, it bubbles and chatters, making its own violent kind of noise, and she suddenly thinks it is going to speak to her. Bright yellow, glistening, spotted with oil, it is heaving gently and subsiding in the pan.

Or rather, she doesn't expect the omelette to speak, but when it doesn't articulate something she is surprised. But when she later thinks of what happened, she sees that really she suffered something like a physical assault. The muteness of the omelette emanated from it in a large balloon and pressed against her eardrums.

But it is not this incident, but the very latest sign of disturbance, on the highway, that frightens her enough to make her list and count up the signs of disturbance, though even then she cannot always decide whether what seems to her a sign of disturbance should be counted as such, since it is fairly normal for her, such as talking aloud to herself or eating too much, or whether it should be counted because to someone else it might seem at least somewhat abnormal, and so, after thinking of ten or eleven signs, she wavers between counting five and seven signs as real signs of disturbance and finally settles on five, partly because she cannot accept the idea that there could be as many as seven.

She hopes this is all just the effect of exhaustion. She thinks it will end when she finds a place to live. She will not care very much what sort of place it is, not at first, anyway. Now there are two choices: a light and roomy apartment in a neighborhood she thinks is dangerous, or a cramped and noisy railroad flat in a part of town she likes.

What happened was that coming up to a line of toll booths on the highway, she had three quarters in her hand. The toll was fifty cents so she had to keep two quarters in her hand and put one back. The problem was that she couldn't decide which one to put back. She kept looking down at the quarters and then up again, trying to drive at the same time, coming closer and closer to the toll booths, veering left toward the center as though she knew that she might have to stop. Each time she looked down at them, the three quarters separated into groups of one quarter and two quarters, but each time she was prepared to put one back it appeared to her as one of a pair, so that she couldn't put it back. This happened over and over again as she rolled closer to the booths, until finally, against her will, she put one quarter back. She told herself the choice was arbitrary, but she felt strongly that it was not. She felt that it was in fact governed by an important rule, though she did not know what the rule was.

She was frightened, not only because she had violated something but because this was not the first time she had for some minutes lost the capacity to act. And because although she had managed, in the end, to put one quarter back, drive up to the toll booth, pay the toll, and go on where she was going, she might just as well not have been able to make any move and might have stopped the car in the center of the highway and remained there indefinitely.

And further, if she had not been able to make a decision about this one small thing, as she might not have, then she might not be able to make a decision about anything else either, because all day long there were such decisions to make, as whether to go into this room or that room, to walk down the street in this direction or the other, to leave the subway by this exit or that one. There were many ways of reasoning through every decision, and often she could not even decide which way to reason, let alone make the decision itself. And so, in this way, she might become entirely paralyzed and unable to go on with her life.

But later that day, as she stands waist high in the water, she thinks that she is right: all this is probably nothing but exhaustion. She is standing without her glasses waist high in the water on a rocky beach. She is waiting for some sort of revelation, because she feels a revelation coming, but although various other thoughts have come, not one of them seems much like a revelation to her.

She stands looking full into the gray waves that come at her crossed by a strong breeze so that they have hard facets like rocks, and she feels her eyes washed by the grayness of the water. She knows it is the greater disruption of her life that is disturbing her, not just the homelessness, but finding a home will help. She thinks that all this will probably come out all right, that it won't end badly. Then she looks out at the smokestacks far away and nearly invisible across the sound and thinks, though, that this was not the revelation she was waiting for either.